Account of a Mild Haunting

by

James I. McGovern

WingSpan Press

Published in the United States and the United Kingdom by WingSpan Press, Livermore, CA

The WingSpan name, logo and colophon are the trademarks of WingSpan Publishing.

ISBN 978-1-59594-580-8 (pbk.)
ISBN 978-1-59594-671-3 (hardcover)

First edition 2016

Printed in the United States of America

www.wingspanpress.com

Library of Congress Control Number 2016932679

1 2 3 4 5 6 7 8 9 10

To Ligaya and Salve

Contents

ACCOUNT OF A MILD HAUNTING

1.

I recall a party between Christmas and New Year's when I was fifteen, a game to determine dance partners, drawing halves of movie titles from a hat. I drew "The Mouse" and looked around as others matched their halves and went to dance. There was one girl remaining, small and dark-haired and looking puzzled by the words on her slip of paper. I hadn't even noticed her before, though she was easily the prettiest girl there.

"I guess we're the only ones left," I faltered.

"It says 'that Roared,'" she frowned at me. "'That Roared.' What's that supposed to mean?" She looked skeptically toward the girl giving the party, now dancing with someone.

"I think it'd be *The Mouse that Roared*. I haven't seen it, but I sort of remember the title from somewhere."

She looked at my slip, then back at her own, considering.

"Oh. Okay."

We moved into the main area and joined the others in the slow dancing of the time, what a friend of mine called "walking around with a girl." She moved lightly, seemed insubstantial, and made me feel lighter too, less awkward. She was a year younger than I but had mature, well-defined features. I got the feeling she was special though others seemed to hardly notice her. She told me her name was Monica.

"How do you like high school?" I asked while we were eating.

3

"Not so much. The crowds in the hallways, I just get swept around. And the noise."

"Do you have a favorite class?"

"No."

"I'll bet you're good in P.E., though."

"Oh, I'm not in that." A hesitation, then: "I take something else instead."

I danced only with her, except once with the girl giving the party. Afterwards, as the party broke up, some of us stood outside amid the new-fallen snow. It was lit by the moon and by holiday lights. There was some horseplay and I threw snow above Monica so it would sparkle in her hair. This it did, but she was suddenly alarmed and ran a few steps away from me. She stood for a moment shaking snowflakes from her hair. Bemused, I approached her.

"Sorry, it was just in fun. To see the sparkle in your hair."

"That's just me. Don't worry about it."

She took a pair of knit gloves from her pockets.

"My mother said be sure and wear them. I better have them on when I get home."

We studied each other, a flicker of something basic, knowing, in the chill air between us.

"Okay if I call you?"

"Of course."

"Your number's in the book?"

"I don't know. Just get it from Cathy. She can write it down for you. I have to say good-bye to her now, thank her for the party."

I watched them talk briefly, Monica glancing back at me as they parted. She gave me a wave and was on her way before I could try to accompany her. She lived less than a block away.

* * *

Sometime during January, leaning back against a kitchen counter, I made the call to Monica's house. A woman answered in a tense voice I could barely hear. She gave a sound of distress when I asked for Monica, the phone was laid down, and there was a brief exchange in the background. A man came on the line.

"Who is this?" He sounded overwrought.

I told him and explained how I'd met Monica, that she'd wanted me to call.

No response. I thought I heard some movement.

"Hello?" I said.

An exasperated sound, then: "Monica's sick. You *can't* talk with her. Do you understand?"

"Oh. Yes. I'll, uh, call another time."

"No, *please*. Don't call here again!"

I had no response, I was only fifteen.

He said good-bye in a disgusted tone and hung up. I was stunned by what seemed to me hostility, something so different from what I'd anticipated in making the call.

I hung up the phone and stood looking at it, not knowing what to think.

* * *

Some weeks later, on a bus returning from school, I encountered a former classmate of Monica's. He attended private school as I did, while she'd been sent to the local public school. On spotting me, the young man broke off from his friends and took the vacant seat next to me. He appeared crestfallen.

"You knew Monica D____, didn't you?"

I must have given him a blank look, perplexed since he hadn't been at the party and had used the past tense.

"Uh, yeah. I know her. Why?"

His young features showed dismay.

5

"Didn't you know she died?" His face began to crumple, near tears. "The funeral was last week."

My mind seemed to freeze, grow numb, refuse to process thoughts. I had to look away from him, could only state the most obvious.

"I–I missed it. I'm sorry about that."

I don't recall what else he said. I think he laid a hand on my arm and went to rejoin his friends. I heard later that Monica had died from complications of a diabetic condition.

* * *

A sort of pall was cast over my life at school, the activities seeming trivial, the other students dull. My grades declined a bit and at home I withdrew, not with my thoughts but with dread. I felt alone in a mystical fog, ignorant of the future but knowing I didn't welcome it. I could only observe, see what came to me, see if things connected into something meaningful, be it good or bad. I was self-isolated.

Since I turned sixteen by summer, I could work in a local restaurant during vacation. I felt no anxiety about working since it didn't matter much where I was, what I was doing. My inner isolation moved with me. Also, there were others about my age working there, some of whom I already knew. I could thus go through the expected motions with ease, observing the flow of people from a remote perspective. When a fellow worker was fired, I took over the "fountain," serving up dessert orders for the waitresses. I liked the minimal dealing with them, the standardized banter, their wearing matching uniforms despite their range in age.

There was a fancier part of the restaurant beyond the part with my "line," which also included the grill and sandwich board. Instead of short orders, the "dining room" had buffet tables with dishes prepared by a chef and his helpers in the kitchen. There was a host or hostess on duty and even a carver for the meat. I had little to do with this area after bussing the tables when I was new. I watched the people who ate there, though, noting differences from the customers in my area, different mannerisms and manners.

On returning to school, I joined the cross-country team and ran hard in practices. I needed to banish the emptiness of the school day–to feel pain, and to delay and shorten the evening at home, the pretense on my part. I hurt myself in a meet once and was urged to quit but did not. I finished limping, then taped the injury and continued with the season. Something had urged me on; I didn't know what. But as I sat with my leg in a whirlpool I felt fullness rise with the heat, a sense of quality achieved.

* * *

During December I visited Monica's grave. I hadn't wanted to before, wary of its resonance, its power to re-awaken my confusion, my shock. But with Christmas break I felt a yearning to move on with my feelings, to put my memories in order. It wasn't so much finality I sought as to be on a higher level in some way.

The rectangular stone was rose-colored and bore only her first name in uncomfortably large letters, along with only her years below, 1947-1962. To either side were graves awaiting her parents, years of death temporarily blank. It was a raw day, occasional flurries of snow whipping about, and they swept now over the headstones and Monica's plot at my feet. I did not cry.

Instead, I saw the randomness of evil in the world, its arbitrary destruction of beauty, grace, and quality. Events soon to come, and continuing through the decades, would prove me right. Whenever I'd see a butterfly, a bird, a young animal or child running, I'd see pure vulnerability. An unending vigilance was needed, a hardening against any and all threats.

2.

In my later teens I avoided social events, didn't go on dates, passed up chances for relationships. Even when introduced to someone I wouldn't follow up with her. It must have seemed some fundamental drive was lacking, but in fact it was something more mental. I'd established a sort of barrier for myself, protective at first but then a source of pride, behind which I strove to be normal and pursue normal goals. Exclusive of emotional ties, of course.

But at age 20, on a Saturday field trip with my geology class, I experienced a crack in my barrier. I was sitting alone on the chartered bus when I was suddenly joined by an attractive woman I'd noticed in the lecture hall. She'd always sit near the front and had full golden hair, curled in the style of the times. She was in ski jacket and jeans for the outdoors, as was I, and as she nestled into the seat I somehow felt at ease with her. She has class, I thought, amused that the trite phrase could fit so. I smiled my amusement at her.

"Ready for some rough walking?"

"Just so we don't freeze."

"Oh, I hear it's 35 at least, maybe 40."

"Thank you. That's so reassuring."

We discussed our impending trek through the state park, the course in general, our other studies and the university. Her name was Linnaea and she was down from Minnesota "for a change of scene." I didn't pry, but it became clear she'd sought distance from some involvements up there. She was three years older than me.

Though the day stayed cold, we were kept warm by chasing after our exuberant and athletic professor. He especially liked finding and discussing strata in rock that were once sedimentary layers. We were often on uneven ground, climbing as much as hiking, and I'd sometimes reach down to give Linnaea a pull up. The repeated contact, my feeling her weight, her abrupt movements toward me, all bred a nascent intimacy under the cloudy sky.

"It seems you're good at this," she said.

We'd stayed right with the professor while others kept lagging.

"I used to run cross-country. We'd often be in places like this. The weather, too."

"You're an 'outdoorsman'?"

I laughed.

"No, not at all. The running was part of something else. A personal thing, complicated."

She was quiet a moment before responding.

"Well, I'm not much for it either. I'll take the fire back at the lodge. Some music, a little wine. But I guess this is good for us."

We traded ironic smiles, then jogged after our indefatigable leader. There was no lodge, of course, but we sat together on the ride back and quietly sensed each other's presence. It was an unfamiliar state for me, though I assumed not for Linnaea. I felt a warm appreciation toward her. I had no idea on how to follow up but, as we lingered back at the campus, we discussed the next week's final exam. One of us suggested lunch at a nearby pub after the test. I'm not sure which of us proposed this; it might have been a combined effort.

When I arrived for the exam, she was sitting near the front of the lecture hall, talking with a neighbor. She never looked back toward me and the test was given as scheduled. I was finished well ahead of her and waited outside an exit door, peeking through its small window in case she left the other way. When she finally came into the hallway, she seemed surprised to see me, but then pleased.

"Oh, yes," she said. "Lunch."

"At the pub," I nodded with a smile.

"Yes." She was quiet a moment, looking away. Then: "Look, I'm awfully sorry. There's this project for another class. I agreed to meet some people to finish it. It's due this afternoon."

"Oh." I didn't know what to say.

"Look. Why don't you give me your number, we'll get together over the break. Is that okay? Will you be in town?"

"Yeah, sure."

"Great!" She smiled, seeming happy at the prospect. I wrote down my phone number and she folded it away like a treasure.

I thought she'd call the following weekend, but it passed uneventfully. It wasn't until Thursday of the following week, the single week between academic quarters, that she called while I was out. She left a number at which I got no answer until the following day. She then seemed to speak in a muted tone, limiting herself to banal pleasantries.

"Did you still want to get together?" I finally asked.

"Oh yes, get together. Of course." A hesitation. "When did you have in mind?"

"Well, I'm pretty much free all the time. Of course, classes start Monday, eight a.m. for me."

"Oh, so early! Let's see, why don't we say two o'clock then. On Sunday. Maybe we can stop in a gallery or two. Do you like modern art?"

"Uh, yeah. It's interesting. Different."

She gave me her address, to which the ride would be three buses for me, though I could walk the final leg through upscale neighborhoods. I felt hollow after we'd hung up, vaguely wishing we hadn't made contact. I sensed encroaching disappointment. I briefly considered not showing, then felt ashamed and resolved to follow through.

I timed my arrival to the minute. There was a security man who called up to Linnaea before he buzzed me in. It was a very tall building with views of the great lake and the city. Her apartment was number 902, near the elevator. The door was ajar but I knocked anyway.

"Be right out!" came her call.

I ventured in and spied a ruffled couch in a floral pattern, and metal-framed chairs with vinyl seats. There was a blond coffee table with rings from glasses and a dirty ashtray. There was no television or "hi-fi," but a good many brown boxes were piled about.

She came out from the bedroom in slacks and sweater, and with fresh make-up.

"Have any trouble parking?"

I explained about the buses. She nodded.

"Well, take a load off." She gestured toward the couch. "I'll get some refreshments."

I took off my jacket and laid it on one of the chairs. Linnaea returned from the kitchen with two large goblets of white wine and a bowl of dietary crisps. The latter tasted like cardboard to me and the wine was not chilled, but I made no comment.

"This is sauterne," she said, taking a healthy sip.

"Oh."

She'd also brought cigarettes and lit up. She offered me one and I accepted, the issues around smoking being still in abeyance.

"I love it up here," she said, "away from things."

"Yes, uh, you have a nice place."

She eyed me coyly.

"A visitor can be nice, though. The *right* visitor."

I was at one end of the couch, she between the middle and the other end, turned toward me with an arm on the back.

"You don't really want to go to the gallery," she said, "do you?"

"If you want to, I can go. Either way I'm fine."

She continued to take healthy sips. I tried to match her, though I was better with the smoking. The crisps were left abandoned.

"So you're still with your family, then?"

"Yeah."

"You like it there? It's okay for you?"

"Okay for now," I shrugged. "Later on, of course–" But I had no idea about later on.

"Okay for now," she repeated. "Guess that sort of describes me, too." She looked around the room, settling on the piled brown boxes. "The thing is, it's all a little topsy-turvy."

I was beginning to feel the wine, which I wasn't used to. I felt relaxed and assumed this was quality: sitting with a shapely, attractive woman, cigarette smoke engulfing us, our talking just a sound effect, a patter. Linnaea moved closer to me.

"It got so I couldn't stand it up there. I was stuck in this office at an excavating company, a job my father got me. I couldn't stand the people, the stuffiness, had to get out. I was married, still am technically, to this guy from high school, but he joined the air force. Suddenly, without asking me. Even before that, he'd be gone for days, weeks, with his buddies. Road trips, they said. My parents never liked him. We had some really bad arguments. It was crazy."

She went on to discuss her girlfriends, someone who was a slimeball, then a doctor who sounded like a psychiatrist, and back to her parents, the air force, high school. At some point I lost consciousness.

When I awoke, the light from outside had changed, grown dimmer, and I felt heavy in my seat. Linnaea was not in sight.

I stiffly rose and tried to get my bearings. I saw my jacket, the bowl of crisps, empty wine goblets, a full ashtray. I warily walked about the room, peeked in the kitchen, approached the bedroom with its door ajar. She was face-down on the double bed, motionless in the half-light, dressed as before. There were prescription bottles on the bedside table. I didn't stand there long, my decision making itself: I wanted out.

I retrieved my jacket from the metal and vinyl chair, quietly left the apartment, the building, the upscale neighborhood.

My barrier resealed itself. I was safe.

3.

Five years after my evening with Monica, again over Christmas break, I met a girl who looked very much like her. She was one of three friends who, like myself, had taken work for the holidays in a book warehouse. She was the youngest of the women, only seventeen, and had lied about her age to get hired. Except for her looks, she had little in common with Monica, so I talked more with one of the friends who attended my university. I'd see this woman the following term, bowling in the campus lanes with her P.E. class. I myself was taking ballroom dancing, the first time I'd danced since with Monica. My assigned partner was slim and graceful, raising memories, but also red-haired and recently married. Still, that certain yearning was being strengthened in me, a desire for quality beyond my reach at the time.

I worked in factory or postal settings between terms at school, where I had to attend full-time or be drafted into the war. The latter would also be my fate upon graduation. To envision high standards of living, excellence and refinement in my involvements, was thus mostly a dream. I had to content myself with the occasional art movie, student play, or philosophic discussion with acquaintances. I took a popular art history class as an elective, and a much smaller class in ancient classics.

I was the only male out of eight students in the class,

though the instructor was also male. He joked about the works and made them amusing, titillating the women, so that I was a passive presence in the room. I was doing well to inject a comment or two each session for grade purposes. When I did, however, I'd notice one pair of eyes linger on me longer than the rest, albeit through rhinestone glasses. As the term wore on, I naturally gravitated toward this woman, talking with her after class and in the library, then at the pub. Her name was Romila, or Millie.

I suppose I became involved with her because of the large hole in my life that was available for occupancy. Though she was younger than I, 20 to my 22, Millie had a sort of protective quality that I felt secure with. She was strongly built and had flaxen hair, cut short and combed to one side. She dressed simply but with token flair. The time I spent with her was taken from my male friends, the ersatz philosophers. She had the same value to me as they did, at first. But then summer arrived and things took a different turn.

I hadn't graduated due to insufficient credits and was again working at a seasonal job. Millie was with her family in a distant suburb, having stayed in the city with an aunt during the school year. My work hours and undependable car limited the times we could get together. This was an incentive, though, to seek quality on our infrequent dates. I spent sizable chunks of my pay on an outdoor concert, dinner-theater at a country club, and other nice dinners prior to movies. It was higher-level living that I sought, however brief my taste of it, and Millie was a willing companion. She didn't exude high quality herself, but was a helpful partner in seeking it.

There were times–in the car, as we were walking, when I'd bring her home–that we would kiss. We'd hold each other, maybe hug, though that was more her doing. I saw this as an extension of quality in our experience. This is what men and women did as an enhancement, a complement, to other refinements in their lives. If not a part of that higher life, intimacy had no meaning, seemed squalid. I was never tempted to go too far.

One especially hot weekend, I arrived while her father and stepmother were away for the day. We had no definite plan, but there was a sizable lake that abutted the development, with boats available to the residents, and she'd floated the notion of taking one out. I parked on the winding private road and climbed a steep slope to her home. The properties were well spaced, at various elevations, with mature trees between them.

"Hi there!"

She was leaning over from a second-floor deck. She wore a halter top and brief shorts.

"I see you're dressed for the weather."

"I was doing some gardening. Come on in, door's open."

I myself was in slacks and golf shirt, and I always wore dress shoes then. I went in to the living room, where I'd previously met her parents and their friends, but where now I stood alone. Millie arrived moments later.

"The air-con feels good," I commented.

"Yes, it's a hot one."

She stood before me expectantly, so I leaned forward and we kissed. Her hands reached around me to hug. I responded, my hands on her mostly bare back. It was brief as usual.

"Want a limeade?"

"Yeah, that sounds good."

She went to the kitchen and brought back two tumblers. We sat on a leather love seat, not touching. I hadn't before seen her this briefly attired. She was trim at the waist, making her limbs look powerful, her bust ample. This somehow provoked a memory in me of employment as an apprentice butcher some years back. It was a totally unwelcome thought.

"What's the matter?" she asked.

"Nothing. Nothing at all."

After some indifferent talk, she raised the prospect of boating on the lake. I went along with her to change the situation. We were soon descending an uneven path past the properties, across the private road, and into a common shore area. The boat house was a short ways down. We viewed the available rowboats and canoes, then stood in the building's scant shade and viewed the lake. Its surface was perfectly calm, with no wind or other boats out, no animal life. Only the sun beating down, its heat absorbed and reflected.

"Maybe this isn't such a good idea," I said.

"A little too hot, you think?"

"Yeah, I think maybe it is."

I was acutely conscious of her next to me–her stark, moist, physical presence. It suddenly dawned on me that, despite our kissing and touching, her hugs, I felt no physical desire for her whatsoever. And I never had. I was simply embellishing a sterile acquaintanceship, a convenient means to some quality living. Except now it seemed much less convenient.

We turned back toward the path and returned to her family's property. I said little on the way, she no doubt thinking it was the heat, the uphill climb. I went in with her briefly to cool but soon said I had to leave, giving some flimsy reason. She hugged and kissed me goodbye, harder than usual I thought, and I awkwardly withdrew.

It was near the end of summer break, so I didn't return to the house but waited to see her back on campus. I then found I was uncomfortable with her, she was a burden, and I preferred my more casual friends. As I sat with one of them over coffee, he suddenly mentioned her.

"You still hanging around with that fat girl?"

"Fat? No, she isn't fat. Just sort of–"

I was stuck for a word. Husky? Big-boned? Conflicted toward her myself, I wasn't inclined to either defend or disparage her.

"I guess athletic," I managed.

This gave him a laugh. I didn't share it, but inwardly I was shoved further away from Millie and from intimacy. I didn't go to her house over the Christmas holidays, instead working every day as a postal assistant. She left a phone message with my family but I didn't call back.

4.

I was working in the first of my office jobs, having avoided the war, and was grateful for the structure it gave me. I was freed for a time from involvement in larger issues. But as I grew used to the routines, the people, I began to look around again and question things. There had to be something more, a higher plane that was not just a reflection of my naiveté. And sure enough, during my first winter in the full-time world, inspiration arrived in the form of a new coworker.

She was physically about the same dimensions as Monica, small and apparently delicate. She was also dark-haired, though more black than brown, and had the flash or sparkle in her glance that I recalled from before. She dressed rather fancily and wore high heels. She sat in the training unit at the front of our large, open work space, almost just in front of me. Her name was Flora.

The trainees stuck together at first, but each blended sooner or later with the larger group. Flora must have noticed my glances, discreet but numerous, and we were quickly on friendly terms. I thought she simply wanted contact beyond her unit, but she continued to gravitate toward me, and I to her. By the time the trainees dispersed to permanent units, Flora and I were constant companions at coffee break and lunch.

There was a decent diner on the corner by our office, but for lunch we'd walk a couple of blocks farther, to a cozy ethnic restaurant with tablecloths and real napkins. Flora would walk slowly in her high heels, especially when there was snow and ice about. I'd sometimes stop as she traversed a patch of ice, assisting if needed, and would think of her as what I then saw: high heels on ice. For, despite her sunny charm and graceful manner, she could be cutting in her remarks and was generally uncompromising.

"Mrs. C_____ is so ignorant," she would say of her supervisor.

"Oh? How so?"

"I give her my reasons. Logical. She doesn't react to them. She's deaf to them. 'Follow policy and procedure' is all she can say. She has no education, just worked her way up from clerk."

Flora herself had a master's degree, which I had to respect. Few people in our office were that educated. It made her stand out more and distanced her from people. This worked in my favor, however, as I became more exclusively her companion. As winter passed into spring, I was giving her rides home, sometimes stopping for dinner. We also began meeting on weekends, though only during daytime. This became more regular when she quit for another job.

One pleasant day, sunny with fresh breezes, we were in a large park deemed botanical gardens. There were exhibits that attracted most of the visitors, but we strolled off to a quieter area. We reached a far corner and left the path to sit at a picnic table. There was no one else in sight except another young couple, lying in the grass at some distance. They were playful with each other and we watched but didn't comment. Suddenly, Flora got up and walked a short way toward a clump of bushes. She turned and faced me, her expression serene, breeze rippling her dress, her dark hair. I was stunned a moment by this vision of her against the foliage. She saw my reaction, held her position longer. She slowly walked back to the picnic table, looking down as if seeking something in the grass, then sat closely beside me.

"You know," she said, "I've never seen your apartment."

It was true, and I hadn't seen much of hers, she having two roommates.

"Shall we go there now?" I asked.

She gave a slight nod. We rose and walked back the way we'd come. It was too early to stop for a meal, as we'd planned, so I drove directly to my building. It was Victorian with a great lake abutting it in back. My first-floor apartment was toward the rear, with a partial view of the water between buildings.

"This is nice," she said, admiring the waves, greenish-blue on the clear day.

"It is, yes." I was regarding her as she looked out. We were standing close but not touching.

"May I lie down?"

"Of course."

She lay on her back on the narrow bed that came with the furnished apartment. It was an efficiency, with sink and stove behind a curtain on one end. I took the one soft chair, where I'd thought Flora would sit while I took a wooden one.

"I'll just close my eyes awhile," she said as if she were tired. But she didn't sound it.

For a time the staccato lapping of waves was the only sound in the room. Then a couple of people passed the windows, headed for a rear entrance. The spell broken, I felt that I should move from the chair, that my direction should be toward Flora. It was only a couple of steps. There wasn't much room on the edge of the bed, but I sat there looking down at her. Her breathing was barely perceptible. Knowing that she was awake, though her eyes were closed, I bent down and touched my lips to hers. Her own lips responded. She shifted to make room for me and I lay beside her. I kissed her again and felt her hand behind my head.

That's as far as it went, however. As I nestled against

her, thinking now I should do this, she suddenly went limp, unresponsive. Her eyes were still closed, but she opened them when I ceased in my movements.

"You're so young," she said.

"Young? But how much older are you–a year, a year and a quarter?"

"That doesn't matter."

She was looking past me, seemed to be listening to the waves.

"So, what is it, then? What's wrong?"

She sighed deeply.

"There was a man I met on my first job, an older man. I admired him, he seemed ideal. He was married and had children. I thought we were just friends. It seemed okay to love him, a secret love, just within myself so nothing would happen. We'd just enjoy each other's company. But it turned out he loved me too, so–"

She closed her eyes.

"Something happened," I finished.

"I had a child," she said.

I was still lying next to her, propped on an elbow, the light from outside grown dimmer. A familiar angst took hold of me.

"A child?" I managed.

"I had to leave my job. I stayed with my family until the birth. There were people they knew who took the child. It went through the probate court."

"I'm sorry. That must have been–"

"Never mind! It's over now, a long time over. I want nothing more to do with it."

I was silent, eased away from her a little. Then she opened her eyes and smiled at me.

"I'm hungry. Let's go have some crepes!"

* * *

22

My contact with Flora was mostly by phone after that day in the apartment. She was busy with her new job, perhaps had found someone else there. I myself was behind my old barrier, protected or prevented from relationships, though I took no pride in this. It was just there, ineluctable. My days and weeks proceeded in pedestrian succession. But then, as the year ended and I went through the holiday motions, I had an experience that I've never dared to reveal to anyone.

It was between Christmas and New Year's, the night of an ordinary day. I went to bed at a normal time, probably around eleven, in the same bed on which Flora had lain. The night outside was frigid and quiet, a layer of ice precluding the sound of waves. I slept soundly for several hours.

To describe the event with complete accuracy is impossible, since it began at once with a deeply felt sense of terror that is beyond words. I was suddenly awake, on my side and facing the wall, aware of a presence in the darkened room behind me. It was very close, standing or hovering and emitting a sound like electrical discharge. I was torn between fear and a need to act, perspiring, and struggled to turn over but somehow couldn't. The presence might have bent over me then, but what I definitely next felt was being *raised or levitated* directly upwards! My terror was almost insanity but I was able to roll and swing out my fist. I might even have snarled.

The presence was gone. A sort of electrical residue fell from the air and I thought I'd seen an outline, that of a shrouded figure, female in dimensions. I'd been quickly but gently lowered to the bed. My tension remained high and I got up and turned on all the lights, searched every corner of the apartment. I found nothing amiss.

I stayed up the rest of the night.

5.

For some weeks after the incident I'd leave a light on while I slept. I'd have wine in the evenings and stay up late, setting the alarm to rise early even on non-work days. At work I embraced routines, losing myself in them, hoping to avoid detection of my inner disturbance. Even so, my slow reactions to jokes and wisecracks earned me some questioning looks.

Of course, a part of me hoped that it had been Monica. Her loss had been at the heart of things for quite a while. And if it were she, I might hope she'd return, that I would see her again. But I was also a rational being, desirous of order and wanting to move on. I had to have Monica resolved–an indelible influence, yes, but not my subjective reality. When my lease expired in the spring, therefore, I moved out of the apartment, though not without a twinge of regret.

My new apartment was in a popular neighborhood further into the city. It was slightly larger, with a separate kitchen/dining room and a Murphy bed that folded down into the living room. I was on the fourth of five floors, most of each floor being a long, straight hallway with apartments on either side. My view was of the building next door.

Though in new surroundings, I continued to mull the event of December, my impression that it had been Monica. Had this, I wondered, been her intention? To lift me out of the stagnancy into which I'd fallen, the personal decline that would inevitably follow? While an aura of fear remained, this view of the visitation tended to buoy my spirits, so I believed in it.

Two doors down from me, on my side of the hall, lived two cousins, Helene about twenty and Tess closer to thirty. I first noticed Tess and greeted her as I would any neighbor. She had a solemn oval face but wavy dark hair, worn longish. Helene was a little taller and also had long dark hair, but it was straight and her face more heart-shaped. She was more animated than Tess, wore colorful clothes, and from the start engaged me with exuberant talk. She also had a boyfriend in the neighborhood, yet it was she who first asked me into her and Tess's apartment.

Tess was at first surprised by my visit, seeming to find her cousin impetuous, but was nonetheless gracious. We had tea and cookies and discussed our jobs, Tess's in a bank and Helene's like mine in an office. There was an old movie on TV which Tess suggested we watch, and during which I unfortunately fell asleep. However inauspicious this was, it amused the two women.

"Now don't go telling people you slept with us," Helene joked.

"Helene!" Tess remonstrated. "Don't be crude."

The younger woman looked down, but with a playful smirk.

"You must be tired," Tess said, and I agreed I was, thus ending the visit.

But it was only the first of many as I became fast friends with the cousins. I had whole meals with them, at their place or when I took them out a couple of times. I met Helene's boyfriend, after which she felt free to visit my apartment, bringing me a dish she'd made or to play a low-level game of chess. Tess was more reserved and wouldn't come past the door.

I was comfortable with the situation and supposed it could go on indefinitely. I could insulate myself with a convenient dual friendship, protected from the demands and complications of deeper relationships. I didn't have a high quality of life in the outward, material sense, but I'd reduced the negatives, Tess and Helene even clouding my unhappy memories. But then life took another turn.

It had been longer than usual since I'd seen the cousins, getting no response when I knocked on their door or called them. Answering machines and voicemail were not yet in vogue.

I finally met Helene in the lobby one evening, commenting that they must have been busy lately. She was, in fact, on her way to her boyfriend's apartment, but there was much more to it.

"Tess has been in the hospital. She had an operation."

"Oh." I was stunned, at a loss.

"But she's all right now, getting better. She just had to stay there to recuperate."

"Good, that's good. That she's recuperating, I mean."

"I guess I should have told you. It was all so sudden—"

"No, that's all right. Uh, I guess I should visit her. I mean I want to."

"Sure, I'll give you the address. Do you have something to write on?"

She was eyeing the mail I'd just collected. I handed her an envelope and she wrote on the back in light, precise strokes. I hardly had time to glance at it before she hurried off.

"She'll be happy to see you! Thank you!"

I looked up and caught the flash of a smile as she moved toward the doors. Then she was gone. It occurred to me that Helene was a beautiful, sophisticated woman, despite her youth, and for a moment I envied the boyfriend. Then I felt ridiculous, remembered who I was.

I went to the hospital the following day, arriving in the evening after work. It was a cube-like building with no real grounds. The name eluded me since I was concentrating on the address, but I suppose it was a specialized facility. A woman in the lobby called up to Tess and then directed me. The building was completely quiet. As I got off the elevator I encountered two young women in a small lounge area, one sitting and one standing. They were in bathrobes over long hospital gowns and the stander was smoking.

"Nice leather," she nodded, referring to my new jacket.

I got past them and sought out Tess's room, seeing or hearing no one else until I found her sitting on the edge of her bed, dressed like the other women. She'd applied light makeup and I noticed a pattern of tiny bluebells on the hospital gown. We awkwardly greeted each other, then moved to an empty lounge area at the far end of the hall.

"I would have come sooner," I said. "I didn't know."

"No, that's all right. I'm fine. I'll be out by the end of the week."

"Will you need a ride then? Some help carrying? I could–"

"No, never mind. It's all arranged."

"Help with anything else? If there's anything you need–"

"No, I'm fine. But I'm glad you could visit."

"My pleasure," I shrugged.

We talked about the TV shows she'd been watching, then about our jobs. I asked about her plans for the future and she seemed a bit perplexed.

"I guess I'll see what comes my way," she mused.

I left shortly thereafter. The idea had been to visit and it was done. As I was about to leave her by her room, however, she gently caught my sleeve.

"Actually," she said, "there *is* something you might help me with. Could you walk with me to church this Sunday? I'll be just out of here and there's those streets–"

"Oh. Well, yeah. No problem."

"Helene will be out with her boyfriend," Tess added, unnecessarily I thought.

"I'll be *happy* to walk with you. Like I say, no problem."

I hadn't meant to sound enthusiastic, just to be appropriate in the situation. Nonetheless, as we walked the several blocks that Sunday, Tess seemed to be beaming, even taking my arm as we ascended the steps of the massive Victorian church. I had not been attending, so the medieval ceremony was at first an interesting diversion. Tess was even livelier on the walk back, and while we had a little snack in the cousins' apartment. All this would have been fine except that, somehow or other, it became a weekly expectation.

Of course, a part of me understood this was a normal course for a relationship, even a reflection of quality in many people's eyes. And Tess herself had many points in her favor, including for me a disinclination toward intimacy. But even between the cousins I felt more drawn to Helene, even though–perhaps because–she was unavailable. Together they'd functioned as a safe pair of friendships, but now things had been thrown out of balance. I had a problem that I couldn't let worsen.

I let Tess know that I visited my family on Sundays, so morning church could not lead to a day together. I also tried feigning illness, hoping to break the cycle, but she'd be back the following week as if nothing had happened. Finally, I got a break one early evening when Helene had asked me in for some reason. Tess arrived from work and Helene greeted her with the news that a man they knew was returning from England, where he'd been teaching.

"He says you should save a place in bed for him!" the younger woman laughed.

Tess was clearly stunned a moment, glancing in my direction, then gave a pained smile and went off to the bathroom. She might have muttered something.

Whatever Tess's initial feelings, it developed that a welcoming party would be held in the cousins' apartment. Helene invited me to come and, though I disliked parties and wouldn't know most of the people, I promised to put in an appearance. Later I realized that the party might be an opportunity for me. I called a nurse I'd recently met and asked her out for the evening of the party, dinner and entertainment implied. She accepted. We arrived with the party in full swing after passing my own door.

The guest of honor was a husky professor with goatee, nice-guy virile. He seemed quite familiar with Tess and assisted her with dishes and such. To help establish my distance from Tess, I stayed close to my date and even danced with her a couple of times. When I had the chance, I cornered Helene and told her we had to leave early, that we'd slip away quietly so as not to disrupt the party. She gave me a coy look as if I were up to some mischief.

After dropping off the nurse, I at first felt great relief, as if I'd cleared my life of harmful complications. I soon realized, though, that I'd opened it to something else. I turned off the radio and drove in near-silence. There was the familiar emptiness, a nascent yearning for quality perhaps unreal. As if in answer–suddenly–a presence was perceptible in the car. It was still, but with its own field of energy, on the periphery of my vision or some other sense.

I checked the rear-view, glanced around. I saw only shadows.

6.

By mid-1974, I was living in a garden apartment in a modern suburban building. It was my first unfurnished place, so I had to shop for a few items and determine my tastes. My one used item was a vintage chest of drawers donated by a friend who lived nearby. He helped me move it along the streets on a dolly, another droll task to accompany moving. I knew others in the area as well, so I thought that, on balance, I'd be more comfortable here than in the city. I put my television in a closet and kept the radio tuned to a classical music station.

The downtown of the village was replete with pleasant shops, including bookstores at that time. I'd sometimes run into a friend or acquaintance there, especially on weekends. There were quality restaurants, entertainments and such to enjoy with companions, and I'd play higher-level games of chess than I had with Helene. My weekends were thus easily filled. There were evenings and nights during the week, however, when the suburban quiet and darker nights seemed to close in preternaturally. I'd lie awake in bed and hear scratching at the ground-level window, which was above me. Cats, I presumed, but almost hoped it was more. I felt a poignant lack that opened me to an involvement I would otherwise have avoided.

Among the people I knew in the area was a coworker from my job. She'd been hired fairly recently but I hadn't noticed her much, it being a large office and she a less striking person.

Somewhat overweight, she had glossy chestnut hair but kept it short in a sort of bowl cut. She had a habit of staring with her mouth open in response to statements she didn't like, a dullard mien. She was called Bobbi at the office, though I suppose that was short for something.

It might have been the gas shortages of the time, or at the suggestion of a manager, but I somehow wound up driving Bobbi to and from work. She was divorced and had a little son, so there was also a side trip to his preschool. Bobbi had a car—nicer than mine, actually–and might have shared the driving, but I didn't want to be her passenger. Instead, I accepted little treats with her and her son, and then the occasional meal. She'd mention having pasta some time–her specialty–but it'd have to be on a weekend since it took more time. I declined at first, not having the empty hours to fill on weekends, but finally gave in to avoid rudeness. She *was* a good cook, after all, and I could afford a change in routine this once.

I was somewhat late arriving, but she'd hardly begun to prepare the meal. Her son was off visiting with his father. I therefore faced a long wait in front of the television, watching a college football game with snacks and wine before me, the jug itself on the floor beneath my glass. I wasn't accustomed to this situation and was feeling pretty good by the time dinner was ready. I ate heartily, laughing and gabbing with Bobbi, though I have no recollection what about. Perhaps at her suggestion, I returned to the living room couch, where I soon fell asleep to the tinkle and clatter of her cleaning up.

I awoke with the room darkened, quiet in the apartment and outside. I may have lain for some time before I noticed the form standing over me. An initial chill gave way to fascination, and my lips were poised to say "Monica" when I suddenly sensed something wrong. The bulky shape of the form, increasingly apparent to my adjusting eyes, showed it could not possibly be her.

"Move to the bedroom?" Bobbi cooed.

I must have stared at her blankly, absorbing disappointment, for some seconds. But I was obligated to speak and so forced myself.

"No."

I couldn't make out her face but I knew she'd be staring herself, complete with open mouth of disapproval, phasing into a sneer as she turned away. Soon thereafter, a loud metallic click signaled the closing of a door.

I lay on the couch a bit longer, my head slowly clearing, my situation looking shaky. I got up and exited the apartment as quietly as I could. I concentrated on the short drive home, avoiding a police pull-over. It was probably about two a.m.

I returned to Bobbi's on Monday for the usual pick-up, but her car was gone and there was no answer at her door. At the office it seemed she was avoiding me. The arrangement was over and I didn't mind, but something about the way it had ended bothered me. I knew the incident had been ludicrous and many would laugh if told about it. But there was also some truth about myself in it that I felt a need to deal with.

What I saw was a potential to slide, not only from the elusive high standards of quality, but down into the vapid, even wretched strata of human activity. I had to avoid people like Bobbi, the human pitfalls, and stay at least close to a refined lifestyle. It was a matter of being cautious and selective in all involvements. Considering the people I knew, and thinking in terms of a relationship, I fixed upon Margrit, a friend of a neighbor in my building. I'd been recruited by the neighbor to help Margrit with a heavy couch, then ran into her in a local bookstore. We'd had coffee together and an intelligent discussion. She was a psychologist working as a school counselor. I decided to call her, expand our friendship to erase the recent fiasco.

She seemed surprised but pleased by my call, and by the suggestion we meet for lunch.

"But I can't make it Saturday," she said. "I have a seminar on community mental health programs. How about Sunday? Would that be okay?"

I readily agreed.

"Or say, you know what?" she continued. "A string quartet will be in one of the old churches about that time. Why don't we take it in and have a bite afterwards?"

I went along with her, though it would encroach on a visit to my family.

"I'm really glad you called," Margrit finished. "I so much more enjoy things when I'm with someone."

I thought about that statement after we'd hung up, trying to "get my head around it," as some say. It was a common enough sentiment, I supposed, yet I'd never quite been conscious of it in myself. I didn't think I was a loner, but the shared and enhanced experience was incidental and rare for me.

Later I thought maybe I shouldn't have called. The music would be in a church, for acoustics rather than religious practice, but still a type of venue I was avoiding. And Margrit had seemed a bit aggressive, something else I'd recently found problematic. I considered cancelling the date based on my weekly family visit. But I was conscious of something else: an overriding commitment to quality including in my own behavior, which meant following through on this. It was only a little music and late lunch, after all, and perhaps I could tap into Margrit's professional knowledge, gain some insights.

The chamber music was nothing special, but Margrit enjoyed it and the atmosphere was good. Afterward we stopped at a regular coffee-shop restaurant. She was pleasant to sit across from, with light brown hair and a face that was plain but welcoming, perhaps a bit sallow. She wore no makeup. She had an average, proportionate build, seemed in good shape. We discussed the music a little more and then I asked about her work.

"It's been pretty routine lately–testing, college info, minor incidents. I have two or three regulars coming, but I don't mind. It passes the day."

"See the parents much?"

"No. Special ed conferences mostly. It's usually just me and the kid, in my tiny little office."

"Do you notice any difference with–well, kids from a divorce?"

"That can be hard to sort out with teenagers, them having tons of issues. But I studied it, of course. There *can* be deep, serious effects."

I told her about my experience with Bobbi, starting with concern for the boy. Margrit freely laughed at the couch incident.

"Weren't you just a teeny bit tempted?"

"No."

Margrit drew in her lips, became thoughtful.

"Okay. And you're sure you didn't say anything to encourage her, maybe inadvertently?"

"I'm sure."

"There was the wine."

"No, I'm sure."

"Right. Well, there were the circumstances of your driving arrangement, the constant contact. It sort of opened the door to something happening. A misunderstanding if nothing else. So you were just a victim of circumstances. Maybe her, too."

"Maybe?"

"Well, after all. She *did* have her own car, and then that special dinner when the boy was away. And the jug of wine– who knows what was in it? She was on the rebound, you were on the scene, so who knows?"

I gazed out the window. It was a quiet afternoon, chilly and now cloudy.

"I guess I should have realized–"

"You *are* an attractive man, you know."

I looked back but she was attending to her salad. She'd simply been stating a fact, as she saw it. I liked her professional distance, felt comfortable with her, decided she wasn't really aggressive. I could ask her about myself, I thought, but in a roundabout way that didn't risk exposure. I waited a little, then asked if her students ever discussed hallucinations with her, or encounters with the paranormal. She gave a short, dismissive head shake.

"Any talk like that and they go to our consulting psychiatrist. I stay away from the twilight zone."

She went on eating with purposeful motions. After a pause, I too resumed but at a slower pace. When we parted that day we agreed to meet again, for dinner. It was a logical next step and Margrit was enthusiastic. But on the appointed evening, as we sat in the ambience of a nicer restaurant, both of us well into our wine, I couldn't really talk about myself with her. It occurred to me that I was facing another dead end to a relationship. But then she informed me she'd be away during her school's Christmas break, visiting family and friends in Ohio. I thus didn't need to decide about her for some time, and so our friendship was reprieved.

7.

Upon returning from Ohio, Margrit seemed to become busier with her work and so was less available to me. I had mixed feelings about it. There was my pessimism about relationships, but Margrit had a lingering appeal such that I didn't want to give up on her. I thought I should temporarily find other company. I'd stayed in touch with the lunchroom philosophers from college but, except for the one I played chess with, I didn't see them often. I decided I too would take a trip, visit an old friend outside my usual circles, perhaps gain fresh perspective.

I'd been in high school with Hal and followed his progress in the academic world. I'd visited him once in Kansas, traveling by train through endless fields of corn. He was now on the faculty of K_____ College in Michigan, a private and rather elite school. He'd been living in Kansas with an attractive woman and I wondered if she was still with him. She'd been bothered by my presence in their rented house, so I kept my visit short. Nonetheless, I cherished the memory of lying in their darkened parlor in the middle of the night, hearing their uneven bed frame thumping above me, the male and female exclamations.

I drove for this visit since the distance was shorter, though I had occasional snow flurries to deal with. My sensation of winter was increased by the stillness of the campus, the bare trees, and the sterility of the buildings as I saw them. I was therefore somewhat prepared when Hal opened the door for me looking quite glum.

He was shorter than I, with a softly strong build, conservative dark haircut, and startling blue eyes. I noticed that he'd missed a couple of shaves and his hair was uncombed. He was in bathrobe and slippers but didn't seem physically ill. I still wasn't surprised, though, thinking one had to make allowances for academics, their totally different work lives. Hal's field was French literature.

"The coffee ran out," he said. "All I have is strawberry soda."

"No, thanks. A little early for me."

"I'll go change."

I looked around the living room, which had assorted litter along the sides and actual piles in the corners. Food and beverage stains abounded on flat surfaces. On using the bathroom, I found it cluttered and gas-station grimy. I waited quite a while for Hal to change and wondered if there was a problem. He came out wearing jeans and a stained sweatshirt, hair still uncombed.

"Sure you don't want the soda?"

I thought I should accept, but I was worried about what might be on the glass, so I again declined.

"So what have you been up to?"

I gave him a brief summary of my job and diversions, throwing in the Bobbi story for laughs. But Hal only nodded.

"Yes," he said distantly, "people can be assholes."

I was momentarily stunned by what I thought a *non sequitur*. I wondered what had happened to him.

"So," I said, "are you happy here?"

"It's faculty housing," he said, looking around the room. "Supposed to be a perk." And he smiled ironically.

"No, I meant the whole scene, the job and people and all."

He looked toward the windows, the gray, still day.

"I don't know that I'll be here much longer."

I waited and he explained that he hadn't quite finished his doctorate requirements. He was returning to Kansas in the spring to defend his dissertation. That should be the end of it, but the delay had been noted by his current employer, making his status here shaky. They were highly selective in granting tenure.

I wanted to commiserate but didn't know what to say. So instead I asked about the woman he'd shared the house with, whether they were still together.

"No," he said, "that ended." No further explanation. "But I'm engaged to someone here. You can meet her later if you want."

My surprise must have shown, but at least I knew what to say.

"Well, sure. I'd love to meet her. And congratulations!"

"We'll have dinner with her tonight."

"That'll be great," I said, hoping it would not be in his apartment.

Later, as we walked around the campus, Hal informed me that his fiancée was an undergraduate at the college, had in fact been a student in one of his classes. The engagement protected their relationship, keeping things ethical, but it would likely seal his doom in the tenure decision.

"Couldn't you just have kept things quiet, met secretly and all?"

"Not in a college like this. It's a soap-opera set."

We spent some time in his office, neat compared to the apartment, and shot some pool in the faculty lounge. A few of Hal's colleagues greeted him but hurried by. Dinner time arrived.

The fiancée lived in an off-campus house with other female students. Hal parked squarely in front of the gate and went up the walk to call. I moved from the front passenger seat to the back, crouching forward to view the couple's approach.

Coming toward the car with Hal, the young woman was indistinct. She was a bit taller than he, and thin, but had a wavering walk and features that seemed enveloped in haze. I soon saw this was due to a pronounced lack of color. She had very light reddish hair, eyes too pale to have a clear hue, and a pallor that brought to mind a morgue. Hal introduced her as Karen.

We drove to one of the cheap steak restaurants popular at the time, little being said on the way. As we were eating, Hal related an incident from his time in Kansas. It involved his road-raging with someone he later saw to be a professor in his department. As he and I shared our amusement at the story, Karen began whimpering as she ate her steak. Her tone was increasingly one of complaint.

"What's wrong?" Hal asked.

"It's tough."

"Your steak is tough?"

"Well, it isn't the baked potato."

Hal simply grunted.

A manager was visiting the tables, chatting with customers, and eventually stopped at ours. He asked if we'd enjoyed our meal. Hal, who had his arm around Karen as she slumped against him, gave the manager a deadpan look.

"Her steak was tough."

The manager looked at Karen's plate, which had little more than the small bone remaining, while Hal's had some gristle and mine had even more.

"You found your steak tough, ma'am?"

Karen gave a nod and nestled into Hal, to whom the manager now spoke.

"I'm sorry she didn't enjoy it. If we'd have known early on, it could've been sent back. But when a steak is already eaten, well– there isn't much we can do."

"You shouldn't serve tough steaks," said Hal, who had produced a pipe and placed it in his mouth.

The manager looked over at me. I gave a slight shrug and resigned smile. Inwardly, I tried to recall how much money I had in case Hal refused to pay. But I needn't have worried; he'd promised to treat and was keen to follow through.

I slept that night on Hal's couch. I'd have preferred the floor but was wary of creatures in the litter. Hal was alone in the bedroom, my presence precluding Karen's. I reflected on the contrast with Kansas: his attractive housemate there, the thumping bed frame, the air of promise for Hal, a life of quality ahead. Now there was this. Could I warn him somehow about Karen? But no, I decided I couldn't, shouldn't. The more-harm-than-good possibility.

I left the following morning. We'd gone out to breakfast first, I trying to be upbeat but Hal seeming to sense something. He was thoughtfully sucking his pipe as I waved goodbye from my car.

Returning to the village and my daily routine was a great escape from Hal's nightmare world. I saw that the desire and quest for quality could somehow be violently inverted. The news stories of suicides and people killing their families gained new cogency, since always disillusion must arrive. I thought of Margrit and saw her in more radiant light, healthily predictable, and decided to call her.

"Yes," she said, "I'm still pretty tied up."

"An upsurge in student crises, meetings?"

A hesitation, then: "Actually, there's something else."

"Oh?"

"You know, back home during the holidays, this old friend—more like a friend of the family—he asked me to marry him. He was rather insistent."

"Ah, I see. And did you say you would?"

"No, I didn't. I told him no. But he hasn't given up. He's been calling even though I don't encourage him. He might even try to visit."

"Well, if I can be of any help–"
"Thanks. I think I can handle him, though."
"Even so, I'm available."
"Okay. That's nice to know."

8.

About a week and a half after I'd learned of the Ohio suitor,
Margrit called and said he was at her apartment. He refused
to leave. Despite her professional training, she'd been unable to
reason with him. She thought my presence would help. I told
her to stay calm, to keep the suitor calm, that I would be right
over.

Of course, I had no intention of rashly jumping in. I called
the village police to report a domestic disturbance that required
their intervention. Only then did I leave myself, not rushing,
allowing time for the official response. Sure enough, a patrol
car was in front of Margrit's building by the time I arrived. I
pulled in behind it.

I rang the bell and Margrit buzzed me in, same as on any
other visit. On ascending the stairs to her apartment, however,
I found an officer in dark blue uniform standing in the open
doorway. His partner was engaged in discussion farther in.

"I made the call," I informed the first officer.

He asked for identification, which I provided.

"So what's with this guy?" he asked me. "Is he nuts or
what?"

"I've never seen him before. She said he kept calling from
Ohio."

"You a good friend of hers?"

"Just casual."

He stood back to let me in.

"Stay off to the side awhile."

The man being questioned was tall but rather stooped in appearance, disheveled, and used embarrassed gestures as he spoke. Margrit was some distance from him, drifting over to my corner when she saw I was present.

"Thanks for coming," she said.

We watched as the second policeman finished with the suitor, then had him sit down. The police spoke separately with Margrit, who declined to file a complaint, after which the suitor was escorted from the building. We watched from the front window as a warning was given on the sidewalk below.

"Think he'll come back?" I asked.

"No, probably not. He understands things now."

The men below dispersed.

"I'm going to have a drink," Margrit said. "Want one?"

"Sure."

She had some Scotch and made us rather stiff ones. We sat in her living room and sipped.

"He lived on our street," she told me. "We were in the same school, our parents knew each other. I went out with him awhile. I suppose assumptions were made, old-fashioned ideas. But I was just a kid, reacting to my environment. He had a little trouble in college, couldn't get into medical school like he wanted, went to dental school but hated it and quit. He got into sales. He's assistant manager now at a farm equipment store."

"He's never been married?"

"I heard he was engaged once but it fell apart. I don't think he's capable of a sustained relationship. Too many inner conflicts to mesh with another person."

"I guess maybe he feels desperate."

She looked at me with raised eyebrows, smiled.

"Desperate. So of course he comes after *me*."

I returned her smile.

"Sorry, my *faux pas*. Of course I lack your professional skill. It must really help in a situation like this."

Margrit became somber, set down her drink.

"Actually no, not so much. It's much different from when I'm counseling others. There I use what I know to help a given problem, provide a service and move on. With a personal situation, like this, there can be issues deep inside, built up over time, strongly felt. They're beyond the professional language, paradigms and techniques and all."

I waited a moment, then: "If there's anything else I can do, I'd certainly like to."

"No, that's all right. Just having you here was a relief. And you were right to call the police. I couldn't have done it myself."

I studied her, noting how she kept her wavy, light brown hair trimmed at the neck. I thought I had to offer her something–now, this very moment–to distract her from the incident.

"I had a situation myself once," I said, "that was, as you say, beyond the professional handling. I think somewhat farther beyond, actually."

She looked up, interested, reached for her drink.

"Oh? What was that?"

I told her then about Monica: meeting her at the party, my impression of her, learning of her illness, her death. I related the effects on my school life and activities, my not dating until well into college. Margrit listened passively, noncommittally, as she might with a client. But when I paused she was sympathetic.

"You were so young. Wasn't there someone you could talk to?"

"Not really, not in any detail. I'd only met her once, after all. And it was 1962. I couldn't be taken very seriously."

Margrit nodded silently. Perhaps she had doubts herself, but I couldn't tell her more–Monica's visitation, her continuing presence in my life. I still had secrets to protect.

"Well," Margrit said, "I'm glad you confided in me. It sort

of turns the day around, the evening anyway." It was darkening outside. "Thanks for everything." And she relaxed in her seat, no doubt assisted by the Scotch.

As I left, she pecked me on the cheek with a slightly tipsy smile. It seemed we shared the thought that we'd just grown closer.

* * *

For several days I went about my routine: work, casual friends, family visit. I wondered about revealing Monica to Margrit, whether it'd been a mistake. To settle my uneasiness, I called her one night and asked if she was all right. She said she was fine, the suitor hadn't returned and she assumed he was back in Ohio. Our talk then turned to ordinary matters until it was time to hang up. I found myself in the same state I'd been before I called.

But the following night it was she who called me.

"I want to take you out to dinner," she said.

"If it's for last week, you really don't have to."

"No. I've been thinking about it all day and I really want to."

"Well, sure then. Great!"

"Is Friday okay?"

I'd normally have been wary, but this was Margrit. She had gained my confidence. She picked me up in the early evening and drove to The Pines, a nice but non-pretentious restaurant in a neighboring suburb. We took our time ordering, enjoying our wine and the breadbasket. She finally settled on fish and I on a lamb dish. We often watched the candle between us.

"Like this place?" she asked.

"Yes, it's quite comfortable. Perfect setting for good company."

She smiled and glanced around. I noticed she was wearing a little makeup this evening.

"Here's to refined tastes," she said, and raised her glass, which I clinked with my own.

"But non-elitist," she added.

"Oh, of course."

"Yet it goes beyond art and music and such, don't you think? I sometimes feel that, if it weren't my job, I'd want nothing to do with the people I service, most of them."

I was surprised but tried not to show it.

"Well, that's not so bad. We only go around once, after all, so of course we prefer quality. In people as in everything."

"There's the thing about being judgmental."

I shrugged and smiled.

"We make judgments every day, every hour. Whether to cross the street, whether to believe someone. It only makes sense to do it in things important to us."

"As in people we're involved with, their 'quality'?"

She gave a vague gesture in pronouncing the word. I thought I should backtrack a bit.

"With people as part of a larger picture, the quality way of life."

"And that's not being elitist?"

"No, it's personal preference. I listen to Mozart, others scream and jump. I wish them well."

She smiled and sat back.

"Still, there's that word: *quality*. Different levels of it in people."

"Language, semantics. The word best expresses the idea. Plus, it's the truth."

"Ah, we're into truth."

"Yes."

"And," a hesitation, "do *I* meet your criteria?"

I waited a moment, then: "Hey, I'm here with you. We're together."

She reached across the table and took my hand, stroked it with her thumb.

"Okay," she said, "so we're not on the guilt treadmill. Fine. Adjustments to people are necessary, but compromise can be dangerous. There are only so many personal options–ones that might work–so you have to be ready but careful about commitments. There's always risk, but less with quality people, in a quality *larger picture*."

Lacking a rejoinder, I could only nod agreement, hope I wasn't in over my head. We had coffee and shared a dessert. Margrit dropped me off at my building, kissing me briefly on the lips. I poured a drink in the apartment, sat listening to music, reviewed the evening and all that was said.

9.

At the suggestion of my chess partner, he and I attended an avant-garde play in the area where last I'd lived. The play exploited myth and classical settings, also featuring some ersatz ballet, but the story and theme were murky and confused. It all just seemed a vehicle for the nudity and scatology which prevailed. The highlight was a "black mass," a nude young woman set before a demented tyrant for sacrifice. She gave a little speech and the lights went out, actors running in all directions from the in-the-round stage.

"She almost brushed you," said my companion, referring to the sacrifice victim.

"Yes, I felt a breeze."

He seemed well satisfied, but then he was one who actually watched people copulate on stage. I myself saw the performance as debased, degenerate. I wouldn't say so to my chess partner, but it was considered high quality based on ephemeral cultural trends. It was basically just exploitative. Nonetheless, I enjoyed sitting in an educated, well-mannered audience to check it out. That was where the quality lay, and it gave me an idea.

I decided to ask Margrit to a later performance. I wanted to see her reaction, how it compared to my own, how she handled aberrations. It was pushing the limits, I suppose, more or less testing her when I should have been candid and open, but I went ahead anyway. Of course, I left out key details when I called her. I stressed the myth and classical references, and praised the ballet performance. She said she'd be happy to go.

"But you won't be bored?" she asked. "Seeing it twice?"

"Not at all. Like you said once, a lot of the enjoyment is the company you're with."

"Well, I guess that clinches it."

As it turned out, Margrit enjoyed the play immensely, finding its shock content clinically fascinating. She talked about nothing else on the long drive home, so that I did in fact–secretly–become bored. But I was also pleased that I had caused this rise in her spirits. We arranged our next date when I dropped her off, the first time we'd done it so soon.

I was somewhat confused in the interim. There was a break in the weather with old snow melting, fog in the early morning. There would soon be outdoor diversions available–visits to nature centers, walks along trails, then concerts under the stars. Was I going to enter another phase with Margrit? How realistic would it be? Quality was one thing, but sustainability another. Her acceptance and adaption to my nature seemed problematic at best. Yet where was I going in life without her, without a woman of quality? I had to go along despite my misgivings. I had to make an effort where necessary.

At Margrit's request, we went to a local pub-type restaurant. It had walls of varnished logs, a stuffed polar bear standing on its hind legs, popcorn on the tables. The lighting was dim, the diners mostly young couples. Pop music played on a distant juke box. Margrit seemed at home here, somewhat fulfilled, as if she'd reached a milestone with me.

"What do you think?" she asked.

"It's nice, a change of pace."

"Hope you're hungry. They have large portions."

"Just so it's not off the bear." I looked around. "They could maybe have dancing here."

"The only real space is in the bar."

The setting was such that our conversation was trivial. I started to drink more than usual, thanks to the atmosphere and ample food. Margrit started to also but caught herself. The place grew noisier rather fast and she stopped eating, suddenly seeming unsatisfied. She then suggested that we leave.

"We can have coffee or something at my apartment," she said.

I was surprised but of course went along. We said little in the car and I wondered whether I'd erred. But Margrit was friendly on reaching the building and led me to her apartment. Once inside, she produced a bottle of cognac, the aforementioned coffee forgotten.

"That's good," she said after a sip, relaxed as she'd earlier been.

"Yes," I agreed, then: "Kind of a sudden exit we made there."

Margrit stared into space.

"That wasn't us, that place. Not tonight."

I let it pass. We were now in a meaningful present and, while I didn't understand her, I saw her as a superior person. I was therefore content to be in her hands. We had a few more sips, then she got up and went to the cassette player across the room. She chose a cassette and stood waiting as it began to play. It was lighter classical music, pleasant to my ears, but Margrit switched it off a short way in. She replaced it with a tape of pop melodies, mostly instrumental. She kept the volume low. When she came back and reclaimed her drink, she closed her eyes and swayed a little to the music.

"Care to dance?" I reflexively asked.

"Yes."

We moved to the center of the living room, stood among shadows since only a small lamp was lit. The drapes were open, but we were upstairs and the buildings across the street were a goodly distance, so we'd only be dim silhouettes. We began our dance, awkwardly at first, then gaining rhythm as a couple. It was like dancing with one of my cousins at a family wedding reception.

"Who taught you to dance?" she asked.

"Someone who said it was just walking around with a girl."

Rather quickly, Margrit closed the space between us. The hand on my shoulder slipped around to my back. I could sense the points of contact with her torso, abdomen, hips. Her upraised hand grew moist against mine, then went limp and dropped also to my back. My left hand wavered in the air. I had to trust her, I thought, trust her wisdom, so I gently completed the embrace. Her head was nestled into me so that I smelt her shampoo. We continued the dance, taking minimal steps, one tune having ended and another in progress.

The next I recall, she was standing apart from me, holding one hand. As I stepped toward her, she moved away again. I again stepped toward her and we were walking together to the bedroom. We each had an arm draped over the other's back.

* * *

I awoke facing Margrit's alarm clock, its phosphorescent face reading 3:17. It took me a while to remember where I was, what had happened, and then to believe it. I checked her side of the bed but she was gone. There was an odor of cigarette smoke, possibly what had awakened me, and a crack of light at the door. Getting up quietly, I went to the crack and peered out.

Margrit was seated sideways on the couch, legs up and back to me. On the coffee table were some of the psychological journals from her shelves, and one large tome. A cigarette burned in a jar lid. I heard Margrit crisply turn a page, then another.

I returned to the bed.

* * *

When I next awoke there was light beginning from outside. Margrit was still absent from her side of the bed. I gathered my clothes and dressed, in no hurry to leave the room. Recalling my own performance, it seemed I'd been biologically correct, with embellishments I'd observed in movies. Surely she shouldn't be upset. I tried to feel confident but felt a nebulous doubt tugging at me, arising no doubt from the gray area in my character.

Margrit was still on the couch, asleep. She was wearing her robe and an afghan that had covered one of the chairs. It was chilly in the apartment, which had old radiators that were slow to function. The journals and book were stacked on the coffee table and there were four cigarette butts in the jar lid. Our cognac glasses had been emptied, but there was also a coffee mug with just dregs. An old instinct made me eye the door, think of slipping away, but again I considered that this was Margrit, everything was different. I decided to check in the kitchen for any remaining coffee.

The coffeepot was still heavy but cold, so I reheated it. I made a little noise getting a cup and Margrit was awakened. She was sitting up when I returned to the living room.

"There's coffee cake in the fridge," she said. "Only two days old."

"Thanks, this is enough."

I sat in an antique chair and held the coffee gingerly. Margrit sat with arms folded, her expression neutral.

"You okay with last night?" I had to ask.

"Yes, I'm fine." But then an ironic smile. "Though it did get a bit—well, fumbly."

The smile remained, prying a response from me.

"It was my first time."

The baldness of the statement failed to ruffle her. She

simply nodded and gazed across the room, lips pursed. I felt her professional self kicking in.

"I can respect that," she said. "I know some people 'save' themselves, so I suppose I should feel honored."

I saw, of course, that she obviously did not.

"It wasn't a religious thing," I said. "It was more complicated. In a personal way, I mean. My individual development."

"Something to do—" She was thoughtful, head tilted. "Did it involve that girl you told me about? The one who died so young?"

"I suppose it did. Does, I mean."

She looked at me blankly, then to the front windows, the emerging day beyond. Already, I thought, she's weighing what this means for her, the shift in focus for her own way of life.

"If you like," she said, "I can give you a name, someone to see. I couldn't work with it myself, of course."

But I had no inclination to treat Monica as an illusion. She was still a real presence to me. Inaccessible perhaps, but still the paragon of womanhood in my life.

10.

My relationship with Margrit receded to an earlier level, a sort of passive friendship. After our critical night, we had only one more date, at a coffee shop during the slow hours. I think we wanted to find meaning, personal value, in what we'd done together–some kind of orderly closure. The concept is sometimes made light of, but it seemed right to me at the time, a thing of quality. I did feel sad when we parted, though, and browsed quite a while in a bookstore. Something there finally distracted me.

I soon had an opportunity for much larger distraction. My chess partner informed me that he too was "on the outs" with his girlfriend, something involving a piece of a pie she'd made being dropped into the garbage. As a result, she'd withdrawn from a trip to Spain he'd arranged, with a large deposit already paid. I was therefore welcome to travel with him while paying part of the cost. I would not normally have considered it but, given my new social vacuum, I assented.

The trip was well-planned and went smoothly, though it was mostly typical tourist fare. There were shorter excursions to Morocco and Portugal, where I felt curious to visit Fatima. It was not on our itinerary but we added it as a day trip. We had a dusty bus ride surrounded by pilgrims from many lands, my companion silently stoic. He was clearly bored at our destination, snapping mundane photos as if scrounging in a scrap heap. But I was inwardly fascinated. The fervency of the people, some walking on their knees, reflected belief in the supernatural that souvenir stalls couldn't diminish. It was real expectation of miracles, though it be as hopeless as the candles that were melting in the sun.

"Next bus out is in ten minutes," my companion said.

I couldn't argue with him. You saw what was here in a short time, after which you were either hooked or not. I could be drawn to the supernatural, but not with the focus at this shrine. My own blessed virgin was in a more ambiguous realm.

Upon returning to the homeland, I was more conscious than ever of the vacuum in my life, both within me and in my activities. My drinking picked up, and at night I'd again hear noises at my bedroom window. Not cats, I now thought, but a shrouded figure, female in dimensions. Her veil might be lighter now, in keeping with summer, with a glow of divine features within. Such were my imaginings on the warm nights that passed.

My melancholy was noticed by Leda, a nurse I occasionally drove about, she being a non-driver. She was sturdily built, dark-haired, and we were at ease together, though with no tendency toward intimacy. Rather, she took an inquiring interest in my other involvements while keeping her own mostly private. She'd sometimes offer suggestions that to me seemed of little use. At this time, however, she must have decided to raise me from my doldrums, offering as she did something substantial.

"I know someone you would like," Leda said. "Another nurse."

We were sitting in a trendy pie shop, one of our little stops while driving.

"You work with her?" I asked.

"No, she's at M_____ Hospital in the city."

"That's near my office."

"Yes," Leda smiled, "convenient for you."

It developed that Leda not only arranged our meeting, but accompanied me throughout the date, in effect a chaperone. She probably wanted to control what was a shaky proposition. We arrived at the city apartment, the second floor of a two-flat, to find my date and her roommate entertaining two men from Michigan. They'd apparently known the women there and had visited unexpectedly. The men soon left after Leda and I arrived.

My date, Nenette, was exceptionally attractive. She was of average height but appeared taller due to her slim, artistically curved body. She had a clear golden complexion with features that were balanced and ethereal. Her full black hair was worn long, but fashioned at the back into two narrow braids that were joined in delicate loops. She wore a shiny blue-green dress.

I can't recall anything Nenette said that evening until after we returned from the restaurant, where Leda and I had mostly conversed as usual. Back in the apartment, Nenette retreated to the kitchen, probably to make tea or coffee, leaving Leda and me on the couch a long time. A certain awkwardness was encroaching.

"Go to her," Leda said.

"What?"

"Go on. Go back to her."

"What should I say?"

"Tell her you like her. Go on. You know what to say."

I got up and walked slowly through a dining room, a hallway with bathroom, to the kitchen where Nenette was idling by a counter.

"Oh!" she said. "Why are you here?"

"Leda thought I should talk with you."

"You should stay there with *her*." She tried to smile, couldn't.

"I wanted to tell you, you know, that I enjoy your company."

"Yes. I enjoy yours also. But please, can you go back out?"

I did. Leda was amused by my report but was tactful when Nenette appeared. A short time later the ersatz date was over.

"How do you think it went?" I asked in the car.

"Good," Leda said. "It went really good."

"Think it's okay for me to call her?"

"Of course! For *sure* call her!"

"I don't know. That thing in the kitchen—"

"No, no. She's just a little reserved. Persevere. Everything will be okay."

I waited a few days, then half-heartedly made the call. Amazingly, Nenette accepted my invitation to see a movie and stop for a bite. She was formal but polite and the conversation was short. It was the same on the date itself, which seemed on the level of two coworkers out for lunch. I was not asked in when I took her home, but she was amenable to another date, which I decided to make more interesting. I took her to a play about ghosts which also had erotic content. She seemed pleasantly surprised by it, but she pushed me away when I tried to kiss her goodnight.

Our dates to now had all been in the city, in the popular area where I used to reside. Thinking I'd try a change of scene, and conscious of Nenette's quality, I next took her to a fancy dinner-theater arrangement in the suburbs. The show was a popular musical and we had a good table close to the stage. Everything seemed optimal. Nenette was even wearing a low-cut dress, which I could see when she unfastened her coat without removing it. A waiter took our cocktail orders and I requested an old-fashioned. The drinks came and we sat waiting for dinner.

"Are you like your drink?" Nenette asked.

"Am I what?"

"Are you old-fashioned?"

Though she was trying to smile, there was an odd strain in

her voice. I could have just said no, or perhaps yes, but I opted for the usually dependable middle way.

"I think that, in certain ways, we are all old-fashioned," I sagely intoned.

Nenette went ballistic.

"What! How dare you! I am not old-fashioned! *Not!* How can you say that? What is the matter with you?"

I think she went on a bit longer, her voice only slightly less elevated. A rough-looking man appeared and offered Nenette hors d'oeuvres. They were plain-looking crackers with a pinkish spread.

"What is in these?" she asked.

"Tuna," he answered dismissively.

She took one and I followed suit, then vaguely apologized for upsetting her. I urged her to relax so she'd enjoy the dinner and show.

"Why don't you take your coat off?" I suggested. "It's really plenty warm in here."

"I can't if you are old-fashioned. You would not like my dress."

I suppose I could have argued for my modernity, but I was starting to feel ridiculous. I let it go and she did in fact subside. She finished her dinner and clearly liked the show, so we left the building in about the same spirits as when we'd arrived. The coat stayed on, however, throughout the date.

I allowed extra time before calling Nenette again, hoping to soften any lingering resentment. I also wanted to feel sure of myself–that I knew what I was doing, that it was *worth* doing. But there was that overarching goal of quality, as well as the time and money I'd expended, that made any doubts about Nenette irrelevant. I would have to push on for lack of a better option.

When I eventually called, she was reserved as I'd expected, but also evasive. She said she was busy, unavailable just now, and didn't elaborate. The call started to grow awkward, but her tone suddenly brightened.

"There will be a party here," she said, "a birthday party for Fay," referring to her roommate. "You just come and that can be our date!"

"Oh. Well, okay."

"And you can also bring Leda. Right?"

Yes, I thought, that was logical. And it was obviously the best I could do this day. So I agreed, then learned the party was over two weeks off. Later, I wondered whether indifference toward intimacy made me overly patient with Nenette, whether others would see abnormality. But there was little I could do, so I waited out the interval and picked Leda up on party night.

"There's also someone else to bring," she informed me in the car. "Can we pick him up?"

Of course I assented. Our third party lived only a short distance away, a pudgy salesman type who'd already had a drink or two. He sprawled in the back of my small foreign car, Leda turning in her seat to talk with him. I had slid into the role of chauffeur.

The party was already going strong when we arrived, young professionals of all ethnicities gabbing and drinking and dancing. In addition to the stereo music, someone was playing bongos and a sweaty young man was clicking castanets. Nenette was quite striking in glossy orange bell-bottoms and brief matching top. Her shortish roommate, Fay, was wearing what appeared to be a wedding dress without the veil. I managed two or three dances, one with Nenette, but spent most of my time lounging with other observers.

"Catch that girl in the orange," Leda's salesman said to me. "Talk about sharp, eh?"

"Yeah, I've been dating her."

"She's your girlfriend? You lucky bastard!"

We actually didn't stay long, though I don't recall how

we happened to leave. Leda might have noted the salesman's drinking, and mine, and become concerned. When we dropped her friend off, she stepped outside the car and I could hear them kissing. I was unaffected by it, confirmed as I was in my role of chauffeur.

Observing Nenette at the party, with her doctor friends and other professionals, I'd felt rather marginalized. Nonetheless, there was the precedent of our dating. I therefore felt free to call her later about further meetings. But I could only reach the roommate, Fay, who'd tell me Nenette was out or was sleeping. As I continued calling, there developed an edge to Fay's voice that I saw was irritation.

"Don't you know?" she finally blurted. "Nenette belongs to the F_____ Society."

"Oh? What's that?"

"It's religious. They take the vow of celibacy. No sexual relations, *ever*."

I was momentarily stunned, couldn't respond quickly.

"Goodbye," Fay said.

"No, wait! I still want to see her!"

But there was a click and the connection was broken. I considered calling back but knew that wouldn't work, might even be seen as harassment. Maybe I could write a letter.

Leda was surprised when I related the call to her. She later informed me, however, that Nenette had taken up with a "crazy radiologist."

11.

The ensuing winter passed slowly for me, the snow and ice accentuating my isolation. The drive to my job in the city became a loathsome burden. I started to rely on "take-out" and "fast food" for dinner, just wanting something to balance my drinking, which was excessive. There were hangovers. I missed appointments with my chess partner, with my family. I called in sick to work. I brought the TV out of the closet and watched whatever junk was on.

Within my alcoholic haze, however, I saw an emerging truth. It had to do with my approach to quality. I had valued it and pursued it, but my focus had been mostly on the *symbols* of a finer life, rather than the matrix which could nourish it. Other people drew on things like work, family, religion, sexuality, for meaning and the definition of goals, of quality. For me, however, such involvements hovered between routine and non-existent. I wondered if there were holes in my character, in my soul. But then I'd remember Monica, almost see her, and feel exonerated. The holes would all be filled.

It was in this state that I turned thirty, considered a milestone at the time. My lease was expiring and I saw no reason to renew it, thought a change of environment might help, and so I moved back into the city. My choice was encouraged by a situation at work, in which I was passed over for a promotion but transferred to an office in a nicer area. My new apartment was conveniently close to the new office.

I developed the habit of taking solitary walks at lunch and dining at one of several small restaurants. I came to favor the S____ Restaurant, despite it's being the smallest and not having very good food. The reason was a waitress, Carol, who was very thin and had bright red hair tied back. She wore glasses and said she was twenty, though I suspected she was younger. I'd always sit at the counter so we could talk, avoiding the main lunch hour in favor of slow periods. Carol would keep looking busy in case her boss was watching.

"You handle that broom pretty well," I said once.

She gave some quick strokes, flashed a smile.

"Maybe I'll sweep you off your feet!"

I was struck by her innocence, her lack of secrecy or guile. It's a different sort of quality, I thought, more basic. I asked if she lived in the area and she said she did, with her mother.

"She drops me here when she goes to work. Going home I just walk."

Another time I asked about school. Was she going or wanting to return?

"I was thinking about it, but Mom says it might be too much for me."

"You mean with your working?"

"No, I have this heart condition, can't get too excited. Couldn't even take gym in high school."

Deep within me a memory stirred: Monica.

"That's too bad. Can it be helped?"

"We don't know yet. I'm going for different tests."

Later I asked if she'd like to meet after work, or on the weekend. She thought a moment.

"Maybe we can go for a walk sometime."

This led to our rendezvous one evening as she was leaving the diner. I had my car, so we drove to a large park in the area.

We strolled about and sat on the benches, watching squirrels and dragonflies, the occasional dog. We talked about nothing of importance but Carol grew rather serious. As we returned to the car she asked to exchange home phone numbers. I assented, then drove to where she lived, a small brick bungalow on a narrow side street.

"Mom might be home by now," she said. "But you can come in sometime after I tell her about you."

She proceeded up the walk and the house's stone steps. It was a Friday, and the last time I would see her.

When I next visited the diner, I was served by a different waitress, apparently related to the boss. He himself handled the register, however, so when I paid I asked about Carol.

"She had to quit," he said. "Some kind of medical problem."

I couldn't leave it at that, of course, so after a few days I called Carol's house. I was answered by her mother, who had a very deep voice and harsh tone. She softened a bit when I explained who I was.

"Oh, yes. Carol told me about you. I'll have her call you back. She's out."

I was relieved to get off the line, thought I didn't want to hear that voice again. Fortunately Carol called me a day or two later. It turned out that, to my amazement, she was pregnant. Hearing my confusion, she hastened to explain.

"It was a doctor who would come in the diner. His office is right on the corner there. You must have gone by it all the time. He got me to go in his office once when nobody else was there."

"Does he know about your condition?"

"Yeah, but he wants nothing to do with it. He's married and all. Plus he's foreign. Where he comes from, it's the mother and her family's problem."

"You could take him to court."

"Mom doesn't want all that. She says just get an abortion.

She's mostly just mad. Do you know where I can get an abortion?"

I told her there were ads in the newspaper, it had been legal for several years, but otherwise I had little to offer. Carol seemed encouraged, however, and the conversation soon ended. I thought or hoped I was done with the matter, but Carol called a day or two later and said the numbers in the paper were religious fanatics beseeching her to keep the baby. Consulting the phone book, I found two or three organizations likely to help her and gave her their numbers.

There came a lull, during which I avoided the S____ Restaurant and did not call Carol. She called me once more, however, and said she'd decided to have the child. Her mother was in agreement. They also wanted to have me over for dinner. I fished for excuses, citing a busy schedule and such. Carol, in her innocence, then blurted out their plan.

"Wouldn't you like to adopt a baby?"

It took a moment, then the picture in my mind was clear: living in the small bungalow with Carol and her mother, and with a child I hadn't fathered but was legally bound to.

"I'm sorry," I replied, "but you see, I'm romantically involved with someone else."

* * *

During autumn I became involved with Rachel, a woman I'd seen around my office. She was another redhead, though not flaming like Carol, and she had a normal build. She was a year older than me and divorced.

It had happened we needed to make a call together on some work. It was a rainy day and we finished the call toward evening. As I drove her back to the office to get her car, I suggested stopping for dinner. She was receptive and spoke of a nice seafood place along the way. After my brush with the social abyss, it was quite pleasant to sit amid candlelight with tinkling cocktails, with a sophisticated woman for company. I was back with my old standards of quality. I felt safe.

I later went with Rachel to art galleries, another avant-garde play, and a sing-along pub she liked. We had more pleasant dinners, the wine flowed. Yet our most intimate evening was mostly unplanned. There'd been an election for president during the day, a Tuesday of course, and we sat on her couch watching the returns. We were interested, making comments, but nestled against each other for the first real time. I placed my arm around her for comfort, then we were kissing. Soon she was softly panting.

"Can we turn this off?" she asked. "Can we go to the bedroom?"

We separated but my mind didn't clear. One of us turned the TV off and we drifted from the room together. We were both silent until she spoke again in the bedroom.

"You can take my bra off," and she turned her back.

I tugged at the little hooks but couldn't manage them. She reached back herself and took care of it. The rest followed more or less normally, more smoothly than with Margrit, perhaps because Rachel had been married eight years. My own satisfaction came from feeling less awkward, from functioning better.

Our relationship disintegrated on our next date. Perhaps emboldened by our election-night tryst, I decided to again depart from conventional venues. I took Rachel to a slide show hosted by my chess partner and his new fiancée. It was attended by his old high school buddies and their wives or girlfriends. Most of the guests were not highly educated, some rather crude, and the slides were of a vacation trip. Rachel complained of a headache afterward, would not admit me to her apartment. I don't recall we even kissed goodnight.

I called the following week to ask her to a professional

basketball game. I'm not sure why I persisted in this direction, unless it was to avoid further intimacy with her. If the latter, my invitation was well chosen.

"I don't think we should go out any more," she said in a firm tone.

12.

Because of a reorganization, I was transferred back to the office where I'd been denied promotion. This was aggravated by a particularly harsh winter entering 1977. Heavy snow made travel difficult, especially since I had to make calls in distant suburbs. The curtailed state of my social life seemed to be for the better. I joined a sort of club in which members wrote letters to each other before possibly dating. I liked the relating at a distance, the exchange of pictures. There would eventually be a phone call if there hadn't been summary rejection.

While visiting on a work assignment, I met a young woman who distracted me from the letter writing. She had a friendly, informal nature and, since she was only a peripheral contact, it seemed ethical enough to ask her out. I took her to nicer restaurants in her area, which was far-flung suburban. We returned each time to her house where we'd talk and kiss on the couch. Her two German shepherds were put in a closed bedroom.

"I don't know," she said one night. "Ralph's father will be coming back." Ralph was one of the dogs. "You might not want to be dealing with that."

"You mean, three dogs instead of two?"

"No, he's a guy. This is his house."

"Oh." I sensed a wave of implications. "But why do you call him Ralph's father?"

She sighed, then recited a chain of transcendental notions I couldn't begin to follow. With her lank hair and wire-rim glasses, she might have been a guru. But she wasn't, I reflected, because that would be Ralph's father.

I made my escape with what grace I could muster, then sailed along the tollway resolved to never return.

I caught up on my letter writing, content once again to relate at a distance. When phone contact was called for, I kept it formal, almost impersonal. I felt compelled to have coffee a couple of times with women who lived within driving distance. After that, I wrote only to addresses at least two states away. This was my main social life as summer settled in.

At work, I had a major problem developing. With my supervisor on leave, I was reporting to someone who'd been instrumental in my non-promotion. She received a call on a file I'd closed, with my supervisor's approval, and insisted that I reopen it. I pointed out that, once a file was closed, further work with the parties required a new file processed in our intake department. She did not care for this and, without reading the closed file, said we should not have closed it. She was a loud, bulky woman who wore bizarre jewelry, and I couldn't reason with her. But I didn't give in. She tried to take disciplinary action, I responded, and dates for meetings were set.

With my life thus in some disarray, I didn't mind hearing from Helene, one of my neighbors when I last lived in the city. Her boyfriend of that time was now her husband, and they were hosting a sort of business party at their home in the suburbs. They were involved in multi-level marketing with A_____ Corporation, recruiting new agents who then recruited others, everyone selling the company's products and receiving various commissions. Helene asked me to attend their party and, while it was something I'd normally avoid, I said yes because she was pleasing and my life was otherwise bleak.

I arrived on a pleasant summer evening as Helene's husband was about to make his pitch. He had charts on a small stand in front of a group of mostly women. There were coffee and cookies available in the next room, no alcohol or real food. I listened patiently, as did the others, two or three people asking questions. The only one showing much enthusiasm was a very young man, probably a student. I saw that Tess, Helene's cousin, was in the audience. We exchanged smiles. I soon learned she was married to the professor whose welcoming party I'd attended.

Socializing was limited after the presentation, apparently so the focus would stay on business. I chatted a little with Helene, but people were already leaving, car motors starting up.

"Could you give a ride to Tess and Alelli?" Helene asked. "We brought them out after work, but if you're going that way anyway—"

She hesitated. I saw no choice.

"Yes, of course. But who's Alelli?"

"There by the couch. Sleeveless top."

She indicated a very small woman whom I'd noticed earlier scrunched between two larger ones. I'd registered then that she was a child.

"A distant relative of ours," Helene added.

Tess sat in front and her relative in back as I drove them into the city. Tess was somewhat guarded toward me, but relaxed in telling of the two children she'd already borne. She and her husband had bought a house in a peaceful neighborhood. When I pulled up in front of it, I thought both women would go in, but Alelli got back in the car where Tess had been sitting. I immediately saw my error.

"So, where do you live, then?"

She named an intersection near my office. Then, "It's a staff residence for P_____ Hospital. I work in the pharmacy there."

She had wavy dark hair that was short but framed her face

nicely. Her features were delicate but her expression strong, with just a hint of crow's feet in the streetlights. She was at least as old as I but more youthful in some way. I pondered this as I drove.

"Did you like the party?" I asked her. "Such as it was?"

"It's an old idea," she responded. "Cosmetics, vitamins, kitchen ware. Recruit people so you get part of their commissions, and commissions from their recruits, and on and on. It's just greed. A pyramid scheme."

"Except they're really selling products, not just collecting money. So it's legal."

"Nobody wants to keep selling. They stop when they get a bunch of recruits. Then they have free money coming in. But of course it doesn't work for a lot of people. Then they're just buyers for the products."

"Guess you won't be having your own meeting. Though you'd have a captive audience, it seems, living in a staff residence."

"No, I'll just buy some products, keep Helene happy."

"I'll do that, too."

Her building was quite visible, twelve stories high at the juncture of busy streets, parking lots on all sides. I pulled up before the glass doors, no one in sight except a guard at his desk in the lobby.

"Thank you for driving me," Alelli said. "I'd ask you in for tea but it's getting late." It was a Wednesday. "Perhaps you can stop after your work."

"I'd like that. When?"

She thought a moment.

"Just come to the pharmacy at 5:30. Tomorrow, day after, whenever you want. Then we'll come back here."

"I'll be there Friday."

"Okay."

I arrived at the hospital promptly and immediately saw

the pharmacy. It was glass-walled and brightly lit amidst an otherwise dingy lobby. Alelli and an older man were within the light, she moving about as if cleaning up for the day. Both wore white coats. Alelli spoke to her colleague when she sighted me, he nodding and glancing my way. She came out with a large carton containing debris.

"Can you carry this?" she asked.

I'd no sooner taken the carton from her than she took off at a sprint down the lobby, which was quite long. She looked back when she reached the doors and laughed. I felt a pleasant sense of discovery, something that would continue into our relationship.

At work, just blocks from Alelli's apartment, my difficulties continued. My supervisor resigned and I fell under the control of a man some considered insane. He seemed obsessed with bolstering the disciplinary action against me. My visits to Alelli's apartment became a sublime source of relief, much more than a balance. I don't recall much of what we talked about; it was on everyday topics, unthreatening. She served simple refreshments and some women from the building would sometimes drop in, apparently surprised to see a man there.

I tried to wind down my letter writing, but some of my correspondents were tenacious. A homely woman from New Hampshire paid me a surprise visit. She intended to stay over with me but I dissuaded her, citing the smallness of my apartment. She left to stay with some nearby members of her religious sect.

Alelli and I didn't go out together often, but I took her to an outdoor concert around the end of summer. We had tickets to the pavilion but the usher couldn't find us seats together. We each took a single seat on the aisle, Alelli about a dozen rows in front of me. She turned around when she was seated, searching for me. I gave her a broad wave and she smiled. On my visits after that, she'd sometimes play the piano in her apartment. She'd concentrate and sounded pretty good to me. Since I was sitting next to her on the piano bench, I tried kissing her on the cheek a few times. She'd just keep playing without missing a note.

My situation at work grew intolerable during the fall. I'd taken no summer vacation, so I decided to visit California, both for a break and to resolve something. An ardent letter-writer in San Francisco had been pressing for a meeting, and I didn't want her following the New Hampshire woman to my door. I told Alelli of my trip, not mentioning the woman, and she suggested sites I might visit.

Though I had a hotel room, I spent the first two nights in my letter-writer's apartment. This resulted in my "third time" and more. The woman seemed even less experienced than myself, yet eager. She was pale with an ash-blonde permanent, stilted in speech and manner, but had hair-trigger emotions. I knew on the second morning that I had to escape her. I sat in my hotel room that evening, a Monday, drinking and watching football. I'd resolved to not go to her apartment. She called, of course, and I feigned illness. She was upset and insisted on seeing me early next morning. I said I'd be in the corner diner. I was having breakfast there when she arrived and berated me in front of all present.

"How was your trip?" Alelli asked later.

"Well, I missed you."

"But it's exciting to travel, isn't it?"

"Excitement isn't everything."

A searching look, then: "You know I'm much older than you."

It was actually only a three-year difference, but she seemed to be adopting a middle-aged perspective while flashes of youth inexorably shone through. She could be playful, affectionate, but always within sisterly limits. She made the rest of my world look badly out of balance.

I decided to resign from my job. When I told Alelli, she showed little reaction.

"Will you be all right?" she asked.

"Sure. I'll always find work."

I called her later on a Sunday night, after visiting my family. We talked as usual except she seemed a little guarded. During a pause I heard footsteps in the background, not hers. They were male, casual, leather shoes on an uncarpeted stretch of floor. I let the conversation end.

Soon after that we had dinner at a bar and grill. The weather was growing cold and, when we left, a raw wind was blowing snowflakes around. Alelli took something black from her handbag and arranged it over her head. I saw it was the type of bonnet women wore in colonial times and on wagon trains, with a soft top and front brim, long neck ties. The style was still in use by certain religious sects.

"I guess there's a lot I don't know about you," I said.

"But that's what makes me interesting. You like mystery, don't you?"

I thought, then: "Yes, I suppose so."

"The unknown, perhaps unknowable?"

I looked over, thinking I'd catch her smile, but the bonnet's front brim shaded and obscured her face.

"Perhaps," I managed.

We walked on towards my car, bracing ourselves against the flurries. I put my arm around her and felt her elusive form. For a while I didn't feel the cold.

THE CRIME-FREE SOCIETY

February 16

I had to walk through heavy rain today for my appointment with the director of continuing education. I wore my vintage dress raincoat and brimmed canvas hat. I found the director seated at her secretary's desk just inside the office. She informed me I was her third choice to teach the course, fished from the college's files of past faculty. This will be different from the English comp classes, she explained. It will be on technical writing, with the bulk of the students coming from the regional carpenters' union. She handed me an old edition of the text to be used, saying the current one is on order, that I should prepare a syllabus and get a copy to her, as well as periodic attendance and grade reports. The first class session is just under two weeks away. I remained standing throughout the brief meeting.

February 19

I worked up an outline for the class by using contents pages in the text, spreading out the topics over sixteen sessions. Before I start teaching I want to meet with Janice, one of my "matches" from online dating. I sent her a "secure email" today with my phone number. I have no idea how it'll turn out. She looks all right in her photo, pale with straight dark hair, seated at a console in her office, not smiling. There's the age difference, 17 years, but she hasn't brought it up so far.

It's going on a year since the divorce. I'm still not settled in this awkward life. The small apartment still feels temporary, like a motel room. I don't identify with the other tenants, can't relate with them, not even older men on their own, like me. Not even two or three women I might have befriended. It seems I have to relate at a distance at first. Maybe always to some extent.

February 22

I had a phone conversation with Janice. It wasn't long, but we have a meeting on tap for Saturday, at four in her office. It's in the capital, downtown, about 50 miles from K-town, so I'll have to leave by three. She speaks in a rather clipped tone, but maybe that comes from working in IT.

In looking through the text for my course, I see the subject can get pretty dry. I won't be able to incorporate literature as I did with my composition classes. There could be a boredom problem like in the old days, multiple people falling asleep. I'll have to keep up a brisk pace, use the blackboard a lot, give generous breaks. I'll dismiss them early to "shorten the playing field," keep them happy.

I really want to do well at this, maybe use it as a stepping stone. Then with getting to know Janice, maybe I can get back where I was before things went downhill. But I have to be realistic. At this stage of my life I can't afford self-delusion.

February 26

I kept my appointment with Janice yesterday. I had to pass a security guard and sign his book, then take an elevator to the sixth floor. The office is large and shadowy with both cubicles and open work space. I found Janice at her console, looking about the same as her picture. The only others in the office were a couple of young men engrossed in some technical problem. Janice logged off and we left.

We had a drink at one of the trendy bar-restaurants nearby. I'd expected to have coffee but Janice herself made the suggestion. She's from upstate New York, she says, and has bounced around a bit. She did low-level work at first, then became specialized when IT caught fire. She doesn't like to supervise or manage people, just wants to do her own thing. She's never been married. She seemed interested when I told her about my teaching, especially its current technical focus. I think we're going to stay friends.

February 28

It's quite late here in the apartment. I'm still wearing the shirt and tie, and the dress slacks and shoes, that I wore to the first meeting of my class. I'm drinking whiskey, in a celebratory mood. I'm still keyed up, my thoughts rushing, spinning about, but I feel empowered, a functional member of society again.

There are 22 students in the class, over half of them from the carpenters' union. There are also a few electricians, a government supervisor, and three full-time students, the latter all young women. The carpenters were accompanied by the union official who'd asked the college to offer the course. He briefly spoke to the class before departing.

It felt odd to be the center of attention again, especially with the need to keep speaking and sound sensible. And, unlike the composition courses, these are mostly working people, not naive, more judgmental. I could see it in their stares. Hence my present state, I guess. But the whiskey will help. And then some sleep.

March 3

I'm still rather stunned from my second class session. There were nine less students present, including six of the carpenters. As far as I can tell, I did nothing wrong in the first session, simply went through the syllabus introducing the course, then had them do a writing exercise. They were to read the book's introduction for tonight. No big deal. Yet there I was with 13 bodies instead of 22. I stalled a bit for late arrivals but then had to start, give feedback on the in-class exercise, then move on to technical style and summaries. I was hoping the hit to my confidence didn't show.

It'll be nice to see Janice this weekend, refreshment after the class. And with the Tuesday-Thursday schedule, I've plenty of time to prep for session three.

March 5

I had a shorter drive this time to see Janice. Her suburb is just outside the capital to the north. The apartment is rather large for one person, a two-bedroom in a newer building that fits well with the area. We went to dinner and then to an artsy theater, saw a strange foreign movie. It was already pretty late when we returned to her apartment, but we got into a long conversation, had a couple of drinks.

The company employing Janice provides various services, but their *raison d'etre* is the security of client's websites. This includes security within an organization, setting levels of access to sensitive information. And it isn't necessarily a business or government entity. After we'd been drinking, Janice took me to her home computer, in the spare bedroom, and showed me a website she'd serviced. It was a discussion forum that required registration to participate, but only the most basic information. It was called the Association for Due Vigilance. I commented that it seemed a standard set-up.

"Yes, what you see here," she said. "But there are second and third levels these people know nothing about."

"How does one join those?"

"By invitation only, then by giving more information. Then an additional password can be established. You need both or all three every time you log on."

"Just to be in a discussion?"

"With a more select group. I don't know, maybe they have some real plans."

"What's it all about?"

"Things going on in society, law enforcement, the courts. I can't go in myself because of ethics. But you can see there's some really strong feelings."

Indeed I could. Bitter, sarcastic, and furious comments abounded, but occasionally a considered opinion popped up. I could see how someone could read past the chaff to select more promising members. I don't know how worthy their purpose is, but it was interesting to see what Janice is involved in. It's too bad my own work is so limited. I'd like to have more to share with her.

March 7

I was down another three students tonight, so over half have dropped only a week in. Stewart, the government supervisor, had lingered after class, so I asked his opinion on this. He said he thought the class was fine and, in any case, the deadline for drop/add is the end of this week. So I guess I'll just teach and see what happens, stop worrying.

The lesson dealt with definitions and descriptions. I tried another writing exercise but made it simpler than last time, then let them go as they finished.

March 8

As I sit preparing my notes, I see outside a man who plays like a child. He's 25 to 30, dressed in discount-store sports gear. He's on the grassy area between this building and the church on the next street south. The man hits a plastic ball with a plastic bat, then runs to get the ball and hit it again, letting out a whoop each time. He also throws a football, running to where it lands and "spiking" it into the ground, doing a little dance. I wonder if he should be out on his own. But there are many in the complex who seem off in their heads. It's the environment to be expected by an older divorced man.

(Later)

Janice called and wants to come to K-town this weekend, instead of me going there. I of course agreed, I'm pleased, but I feel a slight pressure. There's the need to make the trip worthwhile for her. At least I have time to prepare.

March 15

I've let this slide a bit. I've been busy, but I still need to keep track of things, stay focused.

The visit from Janice was quite interesting, for both of us I think. We spent a long time in the antique mall, then had a nice dinner. The town didn't seem too dead since it was Saturday. I suggested a movie but Janice wanted to come back here, the apartment. We talked a long time, sipping wine, and she seemed really curious about me, my opinions and such. I explained at one point that I'm not very political, or religious for that matter, but she said that neither was she.

"I think about things–issues–from a practical angle. Pragmatic, I guess it's called."

"That wouldn't apply to everything, though. Would it?"

"No, of course not. And I can see compromise. But so often the agonizing, ranting about things, could be cut short by drawing a line, facing cold facts, using practical solutions."

I couldn't argue with her. I myself avoid most of the news shows, the biased and repetitive gibberish. I wanted to talk more about her personally, but she didn't seem to know herself real well, like what she wanted for the future. Then it got late and there was the night to think about.

My class has apparently stabilized at eight students. We're into report writing and I gave the first written assignment. Memos and letters will be next. I may have to do a bit on grammar, judging from the in-class exercises. I'll see how the assignments turn out.

March 16

Miss Dudley, the only remaining female student, asked to speak with me after class. She said she wasn't comfortable in the room before I arrived to teach. She wouldn't say why. She asked if she could arrive late for the remaining sessions, to ensure she wasn't with only the male students. I didn't think I should consent to this, so I said she could wait in the nearby lunchroom, that I'd meet her there on my way to class. She accepted this. I don't know who might have been bothering her. Hallman is rather outspoken, but he seems good-natured and is a good class participant.

March 17

Janice called and asked if we could get together Sunday instead of Saturday. There's some sort of backlog at work that requires her presence there. I of course agreed, but I noticed something in her voice that I hadn't heard before, a sort of edge as if she's not sure about me, or thinks she sees something in me. But she's probably tired and tense from her job, and of course that could make her sound different.

March 21

The man who plays like a child has been trying to juggle a soccer ball today. He persists but makes little progress. His problem seems to be that he tries the more complicated, difficult moves without first mastering the basic ones. He wants instant stardom. When using the basketball hoop in the church parking lot, he throws up long "bricks" without ever working on his shooting technique.

I saw Janice on Sunday, as planned. It turns out she has some interest in the Association for Due Vigilance, that website she serviced. To get around ethical issues, she uses a fictional persona to participate in the discussions. Except it isn't quite fictional. It's strongly based on me. She says she needed to make it believable so it can advance to the inner circles. She didn't use my contact info, fortunately, instead establishing a new email account and P.O. box. If they ask for a phone number she'll use some answering service. I was surprised by all this but decided to stay my reaction. Janice was a little embarrassed but I said not to worry, everything's the same between us.

March 24

As I arrived at class last night with Miss Dudley, an argument was raging between Hallman and Covington, the eldest of the remaining carpenters. It involved some issue from a union meeting earlier in the day, apparently unresolved. Things settled down outwardly but there remained a charged atmosphere. It was a bad night for this because, besides the midterm review, I was giving detailed feedback on their first two papers, which were terrible. Yet I had to tread lightly. Perhaps I should carry videos to show in situations like this.

Regarding the papers, I'm especially concerned about Lone Tree. He submitted both assignments on pages ripped from a small spiral notebook. His brief text was hand printed in pencil with continuous errors in spelling, grammar, etc., and no paragraphing. I intend to give at least a "C" to all who finish the course, for my sake as much as theirs, but Lone Tree could put me on shaky grounds ethically.

March 27

Janice and I went to a party Saturday given by a coworker of hers. I spent most of the time watching basketball on television with a couple other men. We left early as planned and returned to her apartment. We decided to wind down from the party by visiting the ADV website, where, Janice informed me, my alter ego had been promoted to the second level. The entry level was engaged in its usual rough banter, this time concerning riot control, with giant nets and crop-dusting planes among the proposals. When Janice entered the inner discussion, however, the postings were far fewer, less emotional, their wording given some thought. It seemed to be about a large increase in security cameras, its economic and other advantages over police kiosks or auxiliary police.

"Want to weigh in on this?" Janice asked.

"No, I don't think so. Anyway, it might not match what you've been putting in."

"I've used a general style, tried to imagine you talking. But you're right. Best to be consistent."

"The topic seems kind of mundane."

"They're conscious of the next level, of being evaluated. They don't want to blow it. Just like us."

She was right. Except what I don't want to lose is *her*. I'm pleased she involved us with this group, because it relieves me of some pressure in our relationship. It's not so much age as traits that have always been with me, at least since the teen years. The lack of initiative in relating, and of spontaneity, easy intimacy. In the end, I suppose, of passion. Yet I strongly want to keep Janice, or someone like her, in my life. So I go along with her on this ADV thing.

March 28

The man who plays like a child now does it with two "other" children, a sister and brother about eleven and ten. They were playing frisbee on the grass between the church and the bank branch. Later they did lay-ups at the basketball hoop. I'm wondering if the children's mother is aware. I don't want to get involved, but my sense of responsibility may gnaw. And I can't just close the blinds. The apartment is too small and I'd feel entombed.

March 31

Another of the carpenters stopped coming to class, so there's now just five of them plus Stewart and Miss Dudley. No one has shown much improvement except Pierce, a tall athletic guy who types his assignments and calls me "professor." I expect he'll get an "A" for the course.

I talked a little with a woman in the fish section at the supermarket. She came around the case while I was inspecting cuts of salmon, which looked good but were bigger than I wanted. She only asked if she could help me, but was rather close and smiling in an appealing way. She's rather short but has shiny blond hair that falls neatly beneath her paper hat. I find her attractive up close, unusual for me, so I explained about the salmon instead of just saying no. She went back and packed a smaller portion for me, told me her name is Myrna.

It might be good to have someone else in case I can't stay with Janice. But I don't see any problem just now, I look forward to her as much as ever.

April 2

I talked with Janice about the man who plays like a child. We were at an outdoor table at a restaurant in her suburb, the sky still orange from sunset. I described the various incidents to Janice, including the latest: man-child hiding behind a tree while watching two young men at the basketball hoop. Janice seemed interested, asked questions, tried to pinpoint the ages of people. But when I asked about what I might do, she just shrugged.

"You're already doing more than you have to, just keeping an eye on him. More than anyone else, anyway."

Our talk moved on to other things. We're both rather isolated people, without close family ties or real friends, so we speak of our work, current events, and the ADV. Janice mentioned a recent discussion topic: reversing the trend away from capital punishment. It dovetailed with the subject of mandatory time limits on steps in the legal process, including appeals. Economic benefits were again a major consideration.

"They seem on the right track," Janice said, "don't you think?"

"As for being against crime? Fighting it? Sure, who can argue?"

"And yet, there are so many hindrances thrown up. A rebellion, almost."

"Yes. Outcroppings of anarchy."

She smiled, and for a moment was beautiful in the soft orange glow.

"There's all those individual points, the issues. But what's needed is a unified approach, a program. A strong organization working for it, with plenty of resources. An overpowering force to *squash* the anarchy."

"Think that's the ADV?"

"I don't know. They seem to think they are."

I have to agree with Janice, and with many people on the website, about the negative forces in society. People trying to lead normal, responsible lives are continually victimized or threatened by out-of-control lawbreakers, many of them extremely vicious. At the same time, there are ignorant or self-promoting people who support the criminals against police, the courts, and positive, necessary values. It's no wonder there's an Association for Due Vigilance.

April 3

I've received a disturbing phone call. It was the security chief at the college. He said the monitor I used in my last class was missing when support staff went to pick it up. That was Friday. Today the cart it was on was found outside in some bushes. I had no useful info for the chief. Considering my students, their possible involvement, I can only picture Sprague. He doesn't participate in class and sometimes seems sullen. He's nodded off a couple of times, once with Lone Tree following. But Sprague does the written work well enough, should finish the course okay. There's just that inevitable conjecture about who it was if it was one of them, whether I'm missing something, being fooled.

I was at the supermarket and mentioned the apparent theft to Myrna. She said it happens in the store once in a while, employees are questioned, this in addition to stealing by customers.

"But you know what?" she added. "Don't get involved. Even if you have suspicions. That's what I go by. I know they say that's wrong, bad attitude, but who's the one taking the risk? Know what I mean? Revenge and all."

I more or less thanked Myrna for her advice and moved on, she having work to do. She said to call ahead next time and she'll take her break with me.

April 5

Janice called, excited. She said we can now join the third level discussion on the ADV website. This apparently resulted from her using my story of the man-who-plays-like-a-child in a discussion. I didn't know what to say, told her it was great. But my thoughts were kind of confused, still are. More and more of my info is flowing to the organization. I'm being judged.

I'll just get back to my course for now. I'm a little behind, papers to grade and the session on figures and tables to plan. I can't show videos any more.

April 10

Leaving the building on Saturday, I encountered the man who plays like a child, who was coming in. I greeted him politely, but he returned only a sardonic stare, as if conscious of some fault in me. I simply proceeded on my way, recalling the advice to "consider the source." It seems unlikely he's been reading the ADV discussions, especially the second and/or third levels.

I went to a musical play with Janice and a couple from the party. It was very long, or seemed so to me, though the others enjoyed it thoroughly. We stopped for drinks and I got a little drunk, I suppose out of boredom, but I fortunately wasn't driving. They dropped us at her apartment and I was very soon asleep. In the middle of the night, though, I was awakened by Janice, who was talking about marriage. I haven't any recall of what I said in response. I slipped quickly back into slumber.

In the morning we had a simple breakfast in the apartment. Janice was in good spirits, though she didn't mention our nocturnal exchange. I myself was somewhat hung over. She asked if I'd like to check the ADV website, something we'd normally have done the evening before, but I thought I should save my eyes for the road. She agreed and gave me the third-level password so I could look in on my own.

Back here in K-town, I've logged on to the site but now feel somewhat disturbed. The Level One chatter was actually better than usual, at first anyway, with ideas about firming up restitution to victims. But then the mandatory-lie-test crowd barged in and things deteriorated. Level Two was into unsealing juvenile arrest records, along with a "public morality" class in the schools, emphasis on assault and stealing. On Level Three, the link between poverty and crime was discussed. Since most in poverty are born into it, the idea was to limit such births. For a family on welfare, no additional benefits would be paid if they had another child unless at least one parent consented to sterilization. Other birth control would also be strongly promoted.

April 12

The class perked up yesterday for the session on resumé writing. But that's the last topic before oral presentations and the final. I'm still bothered by the thought that nobody has learned much of anything, what that says about me as a teacher. And I've caught myself straining, my throat a little tight, my voice getting hoarse. I must relax.

April 13

A rather jarring phone call from Janice. An email was received from the ADV at the special address she established. It seems there's to be an actual, physical, meeting of select Level Three members (in effect, a fourth level) at a location in the capital. The meeting is just over two weeks off. I (my ADV self) am expected to attend. Janice seemed entranced by the proposition, somewhat breathless. I didn't know what to say, humored her. I finally changed the subject to our coming weekend.

April 17

I had my weekend with Janice but wasn't able to enjoy it. I was more than ever aware of my need for her, or someone like her, in my situation and stage of life. And I've come to feel close to her, to love her. But I'm conflicted. A big part of our relationship, the bonding agent really, has been the ADV. We've gotten more and more involved and I've been carried along by Janice's enthusiasm. Honestly, I think, not pretending. And I still find her spirit a beautiful thing. But I don't think our relationship should depend on that organization, its approval of us (the fictional me). So I gently suggested that maybe we should rein in our participation, draw the line at in-person contacts like the impending conference. She was taken aback, seemed mystified.

"But you believe in them, don't you? What they stand for and all?"

"Yes, of course. Basically."

"And the work I've put in, pushing you along. And you're so far in. You can really be a part of things, have a say about what happens."

"Believe me, I'm grateful. I think it's great we've been involved in this. I'm just saying, you know, that being there with them in person is a whole different thing. And it would just be me there, not *us*."

"Well, I'd go there myself if I could, but you know I can't. And I'll be there in spirit with you. You know that too."

In the end she asked me to do it for *her*, if no other reason, and of course I said yes. What else could I do? I couldn't face the abyss of losing her, so I said what I had to say. And it was all Janice wanted to hear, changing quickly to an upbeat mood. We took a drive later past the venue for the meeting. It's an older banquet hall, not big, on a wide street of mostly big old houses. The street is the first major one east of Meridian, which continues off the highway from K-town and runs through the heart of the capital. The meeting site will be easy to find for those invited.

April 19

The agenda for the ADV conference arrived via email at Janice's special address. She forwarded it to me. The featured subject is preemptive surgery to arrest aggression in actual and potential criminals. There will also be a discussion of scientific questioning, using injections and such, to obtain truthful statements. Legal, financial, and political matters will be covered in committees. I wish I could be someone else for a day, or walk through invisible, see and hear the conference without committing my true self, my physical identity, to ADV activity. But there's just the one option if I hope to keep Janice, which I do.

I need to get a final exam together for the class tomorrow. Maybe I'll just have them write about their thoughts on the course, using some of the elements of technical writing they were supposed to learn.

April 23

Back from the visit to Janice. We were fairly relaxed, the issue of the conference out of the way, but there was an edge to things. Maybe it was that proposal of anti-aggression surgery. We didn't discuss it, but we're both conscious of it. Level Three on the website was just a bland discussion of enhancements to home confinement.

I need to finish grading the final exam, compute the course grades. I'll submit the sheet to the director of continuing education, with a copy to the union official on the carpenters only.

April 24

I've finished my grading and computing, so I can submit my reports on the course. I'll also mail the postcards the students addressed on the last day, giving each of them his/her grade:

> Covington ...... A
> Dudley .... A
> Hallman .... A
> Lone Tree C
> Pierce .... A
> Sprague .... B
> Stewart .... A

The report sheet lists all 22 students who started the course, so I'm listing 15 of them as "withdrew." I don't actually know how many went through the process. I only know they stopped showing up.

I know I'm being generous in the grading, but being objective would show the course to be a failure, not to mention my teaching.

April 26

I had a beer with Myrna on her lunch break from the store. We were in a neighborhood restaurant that has a beer-and-wine license. I asked what she thought about our law enforcement and the justice system, how effective they are. Whether crime might be gaining the upper hand. She mulled it over a moment.

"Well, of course there's a lot of baddies out there. No doubt about that. But there's things folks can do themselves, know what I mean? Keep everything locked, look out for each other, know where you walk, and of course there's the gun. Not for everyone, I guess, but in the end it's the equalizer. A dog or two can help, and then there's alarm systems."

"What about the police and the courts?"

"Problem there is the delay. Police are usually around after the fact, and the courts have been ruined by politicians. Things never end."

"Maybe they can be improved, tightened up."

"I hear about that sometimes. Reform. Change an organization or something so it's better. Problem is, the thing you change it to starts going downhill the minute you walk away. It's in the nature of things, of human activity."

We moved on to lighter subjects. We were there for a little enjoyment, after all, to get to know each other. I don't foresee where it might lead.

April 28

Talked awhile with Janice on the phone. I wasn't surprised she called, and in fact would've called myself since the conference is tomorrow. But I was a little taken aback–not unpleasantly–by her tone of reverence toward the conference and me as a participant. There wasn't really much to discuss, we were mostly just venting our anticipation, mostly hers. She'll be working at her office tomorrow while I'm with the ADV.

I'm feeling quite relaxed, unexpectedly so. It wasn't so much the call since I was starting to loosen up earlier. Maybe I'm just resigned, as if I have no control over things. But that isn't good really, is it?

April 29

The old banquet hall is located on a corner, with its own modest parking area. I parked on the street, however, the major one in front, where there's plenty of space fronting the big old houses. I didn't want to get blocked in, or to be conspicuous, in fact I was hiding. I wanted to see who else was arriving, what kind of people they were. This from my cozy vantage point across the wide avenue. I'm not there now, I'm in a coffee shop a few blocks away.

The people going in were largely in their 40s and 50s, about three-quarters men, with some ethnic diversity. Since it's Saturday, most were casually dressed, though no one looked sloppy. I was somewhat surprised that many seemed to know each other, even arriving in twos and threes. There was one man I recognized, a congressman or state representative I've seen briefly on TV. He was wearing a suit and walked in-between two other men. No doubt there was security inside, checking passwords or invitations or both. A printout of my invitation was in my pocket.

But I was comfortable in the car, observing, not really wanting to join the parade into the banquet hall. I don't like crowds, big groups, being confined with them. The party with Janice's friends was bad enough, but this is on a whole new level. I tend to go along with things, or pretend to, but there's a limit. I could try forcing myself, just to keep Janice, but I've been forcing myself in other things, like teaching, and it hasn't worked out. Unnatural effort does not achieve good results.

So here I am in the coffee shop, an increasingly tardy member of the Association for Due Vigilance, fourth level.

(Later)

I'm back in K-town, in my apartment. As I was parking in the lot, I saw the man who plays like a child coming from a nearby strip mall. He was carrying a soft drink cup, which he would raise every few steps to gain traces of flavor from the ice within. He noticed me watching from where I stood beside my car. His look then was one of defiance, as if cognizant of my thoughts and their transmission to others. He continued into the building without taking further swigs. I had not greeted him.

Janice will still be at work, thinking I'm at the conference which is still in progress. I'll call her apartment and leave a message on the machine, explain that I could not go in.

(Still Later)

I'm in an out-of-state motel. I decided to make a trip to visit relatives. I've called my apartment to check for messages, using the remote feature, but there was only a telemarketing pitch. Nothing from Janice. I don't have access to the Internet here, but I checked it before I left.

There was a message today from Miss Dudley. She thanked me for a "wonderful experience," said she hoped to have me as a teacher again.

CANDIDATE FOR A FOOTNOTE

1.

I was surprised at receiving a call that an old friend, whom I'll call Thomas, had passed away. Not because of his age, for he was older than myself and I've been retired for some years. I was surprised because the caller had been his wife, she said, and I'd never known she existed. This and because Thomas had been a monk since his teenage years.

"It's a little complicated," she said. "I can explain it when I see you in person. If you're able to come, I mean."

"Yes, of course. When is the funeral?"

"It was last week."

"Oh."

"Actually, he's buried back at the monastery. But there's legal stuff involving his estate, especially the house here. We need to protect it from the Order."

"The order of monks?"

"Yes."

"All right. But how does that involve me?"

"He left you a few things, one of them sealed. It might be important. The lawyer thinks you should be present so we can do everything at once."

"Who's the lawyer?"

"Mr. R____. He's here in town, an old friend of Tom's family. He's handling things for free."

I agreed to make the trip. My time was entirely my own, so I told the caller, Sandra, that I'd leave the next day. It'd be a long drive, across the better parts of two states, so I curtailed my evening and got a good rest. With this and my aroused curiosity, I held up well against the distance and the monotony of endless cornfields.

The house was on the edge of a quiet town with many shuttered businesses. It was large and red brick with a full second level and partial third. The grounds were well-kept but had a dry, windswept appearance like the rest of the town. I climbed the stone steps and rang the bell, which was answered rather quickly by a woman in her fifties. She had calm features behind rimless glasses, light brown hair worn longish. We exchanged greetings and she ushered me in. I sat in a large living room furnished with items from many decades. Sandra offered coffee, I accepted, and she called back to someone in another room. Then she joined me.

"There's quite a history to this house," she said, "as you can see."

She gestured toward the many portraits on the walls, individual and group. I spotted a few of Thomas, younger in age, and Sandra herself with an elderly woman.

"I was his mother's live-in nurse," she explained. "It went on a long time. She died a few years ago."

Our coffee was brought in by a woman in her thirties, dark-haired and a little stocky. She walked with a pronounced limp emanating from her hip.

"This is my helper, Natalya."

We exchanged pleasantries but the younger woman remained standing. She then withdrew as if preoccupied.

"She's been a treasure," Sandra said. "Even before, Tom's visits were few and far between."

"Has Natalya been with you long?"

"Since shortly after his mother died, around the time we were married."

I nodded, then: "I never knew."

"Almost no one did. It had to be secret. He was attached to the monastic life, his trips away from it, a lifestyle he was settled in. But we had to be married once his mother died. The house passed to him but the Order could grab it if he was sole owner. And he wasn't about to leave them. So we got married as a safeguard."

"Well, you're in the clear now, aren't you? He *has* left the Order, in effect, so they have no further claim to his property."

"The thing is, there's that short time between his mother's death and our marriage. She was still down as owner until we changed the deed, but you never know. Mr. R_____ says he can handle it, but I should be down as sole owner as soon as possible."

"I see. Well, I'm ready to do my part. Is there anyone else involved?"

"Only Natalya. The lawyer said he could make it tonight if you were here, so I guess I'll give him a call. Can you stay for supper?"

"Thank you, yes. But I need to arrange a place to stay tonight."

"You're welcome to stay here. As you've probably noticed, we have plenty of room."

I hesitated out of courtesy, but then gladly accepted her offer. To stay a night in Thomas's home–his real home, not the monastery–would be a fitting end to our earthly friendship.

* * *

The lawyer, Mr. R_____, arrived promptly as we were finishing supper. It had been a simple meal with little conversation. Sandra seemed quite straightforward, matter-of-fact, but Natalya was somewhat uneasy with my presence. I assumed it was due to my disrupting their routine. The lawyer's arrival dispelled the tension, however, so he was doubly welcome.

He was an elderly man who had scaled back his practice, which had always been mostly local. However, he set about his work with energy and good humor, settling into a vacant place at the table while it was still being cleared. There weren't so many papers involved, but he was punctilious in their sorting, arrangement, and distribution, no doubt a reflection of long-held work standards.

What it came down to was this: Thomas had left all his property to Sandra, except for a few small items to Natalya and myself. Natalya received a collection of religious medals and statuary that Thomas had accumulated over the years. Some of it was very old, perhaps valuable. I was left a cigar box of childhood memorabilia and a sealed brown envelope, nine by twelve inches, with flexible contents. No other people or organizations were mentioned in the statement. Mr. R_____ obtained our signatures, affixed his own, and declared the day's business to be finished.

"Shall we have a small toast?" Sandra offered.

No one objected, so she brought out a liqueur bottle and small glasses, green-tinted. The toast was to Thomas, of course, Sandra offering it, and I felt some camaraderie with the others in remembering my old friend. It wasn't a time for storytelling, though, just reflection. When Sandra asked if anyone would like another, I said yes.

"Me too," Natalya added.

It was then, as we drank together, that it suddenly hit me about her. The same width in her face, the color of hair and eyes, but most of all the relaxed, dreamy look as she savored the alcoholic beverage. Many were the nights I viewed that face, that expression, as Thomas and I shared in the fellowship of the cups.

* * *

My room for the night was quite spacious, though with dated furniture again and mustiness in the air. I wasn't especially tired, despite the long day, so I sat up reflecting awhile. This had been Thomas's home, his heritage, the place that had nurtured a soul I could relate to, of which there are few. Now there was Natalya, a living secret, one that I would keep because it was demanded–for now–by the situation. And yet she was testimony to Thomas, his ability to live beyond his niche. Testimony to his transcendence.

I sifted through the cigar box, smiled at the predictability of children's treasures, at least a half-century ago. Favorite marbles, arrowheads, foreign coins, baseball cards that are probably worth a fortune now. There were also a good many gears from small machines, their various colors suggesting various component metals. Their appeal as mementos escaped me but, as Thomas himself was fond of saying, there's no explaining human tastes.

All of which left the sealed packet, labeled only with my name and "His Eyes Only." I held it a minute or two before slitting it open, wanting to absorb my friend's confidence, the final bond between us. Then the envelope was open, my hand withdrawing a thin sheaf of papers, a single short manuscript, neatly typed. I settled comfortably in my chair, drew the lamp closer, and concentrated on the words of my departed friend.

2.

Thomas's Narrative

When President Kennedy came to Chicago in 1962 to back a candidate for the U.S. Senate, I had an unusual opportunity to speak with him. I was asked by a priest at my school to accompany him, along with another priest and another prep seminarian, to a reception for the president. My mentor had gotten passes from another priest in the area, a celebrity of sorts for his work with troubled youth. As we rode to the event in a stodgy seminary car, we were excited but also complacent, as if we were collecting a fringe benefit of our roles in society. We should have felt a sense of urgency, considering later events, but only I was to get a hint of them that night.

As we arrived in the anteroom, my mentor was greeted by the celebrity priest, who had work assignments for us students. Mine was to check passes out at the entrance, while my colleague had duties in the reception hall itself. Naturally, I was disappointed, suspecting as time passed that I'd miss meeting Kennedy. But I was suddenly approached by one of the burly men who'd been patrolling the area.

"I'll take over, Junior. Go grab yourself a ginger ale."

While seeking a washroom on my way to the reception hall, I almost passed a small office or storeroom with the door ajar. While the light inside was weak, I could clearly see the president sitting with his legs crossed, no one else in the room. I was motionless and stared, not knowing what to do or say, but he quickly noticed me.

"Hi, there. Come on in."

He only half-smiled, his eyebrows raised. It wasn't an expression I'd seen on him before. He then peered intently at me and his smile widened.

"You resemble someone from my school days. We had some great times. As you do now, I imagine."

"I'm in the seminary."

"Ah, the seminary. Well, have a seat. I don't often get to talk with seminarians."

I sat facing him in a semi-upholstered hotel chair. Having an instant to reflect, I wondered if I were dreaming this.

"Is this all right, my being here? Aren't you busy?"

"Security alert. I can't go in yet."

"Security? I was checking passes. I hope I didn't–"

The president chuckled, putting me at ease.

"No, this is something else. The boys are clearing it up."

One of them poked his head in, eyed me quizzically.

"Everything all right, sir?"

Kennedy gave a dismissive wave.

"Catching up on Church doctrine," he said.

The man withdrew. I heard the word "choirboy" mumbled in the passageway, assumed they were referring to me. My companion was listening, too, gazing between me and the door.

"Does it have to do with Khrushchev?" I blurted, the fears of my Cold War childhood finding vent.

The president laughed with an abrupt stop.

"He's just a bad-tempered old Buddha. Totally out of place. He's a farmer, actually, of peasant origins. I suspect he'd like to return there."

"But, the spread of communism–"

"Yes, well, we're already stuck in Korea. We can't expand

our commitment in Vietnam, though. We need to start limiting our military involvements so we can focus on domestic priorities. Of course, there will always be opposition to this. People make money on war and weaponry, and it blinds them to certain realities."

"That was our debate topic last year, disarmament. But it was mainly nuclear weapons."

"Is that with the National Forensic League?"

"Yes."

"Great organization. Anyone bring up a tie-in with the oil industry?"

His eyes were alert, really interested. I sensed a great mind at work and felt diminished.

"No. Natural resources is a subject for the speech events. It's completely separate from arms limitation."

His classic full smile appeared for the first time. He followed with his full laugh, not stopping short as before, but then noticed my puzzlement.

"Don't ever believe it," he said.

I was probably frowning then, begging an explanation.

"The oil companies want to regain some of the power they lost to OPEC. They can do it by making oil, and maybe other resources, an issue in war. The same people and organizations who control big oil also control the arms industry. They're organized internationally, placing themselves above the law of any country. You know of the Hiss case?"

"Tried for spying? Or for being a communist?"

"Along those lines. But prior to World War II, he was our government's control on the financing of arms buildups abroad. This earned him some big enemies among our financiers. It was then that his accuser, Chambers, began approaching him in public, having photos taken and such. It created a guilt-by-association case that could be sprung at any time."

"Wasn't Mr. Nixon part of the prosecution?"

"Yes, my worthy opponent. The arms and oil financiers can work through our government, besides having their international organizations. They prefer contacts who work independently, even secretly. So it sometimes happens that we have public servants working for private interests."

"You mean the military-industrial complex?"

Kennedy smiled sadly.

"If it stopped at that, we could control it. The problem comes when they work *at the same time* for private profit and our government. Then we're the pawns of profiteers, such as big oil. You followed the Bay of Pigs developments?"

"Yes, but didn't you authorize that?"

"When it was already moving, yes. The CIA planned it in later '60, while Ike was packing his golf clubs. Things were well along by the time I was filled in. Yet people outside government were in the know, including an oil company, Zapata–have you heard of them?"

"No." He had actually pronounced it "Zapotter."

"Offshore drilling. Not far from Cuba itself, actually. Someone from there has a tie with the CIA–a de facto agent. But the controlling loyalty is to profit, and if war results they profit from that, too. We have to be vigilant or our future will be decided by big oil, the arms industry, and the financiers behind them."

"Can they be stopped?"

"They're organized internationally, without morality or ethics as you and I know them. They were behind the attempt to assassinate de Gaulle. We'll have to work with other countries, whatever their politics, to head off the threat to our people's futures. But we'll focus our efforts here, where we have the authority, and I plan to do it before my term is done."

He'd fallen stonily serious, his eyes set and piercing in a way they never photographed. He quickly became conscious of his intensity, relaxing with a bemused smile, and asked what I'd been reading lately. We started discussing J. D. Salinger but one of the burly men soon came in with the celebrity priest.

"Green light, Mr. President."

In the reception hall he became the Kennedy everyone was used to, smiling and confident, his erect posture exaggerating his height and strength. There was no further signal of anything sinister, only an inspired and grateful knot of humanity basking in the president's charisma. For me, however, the tight nerves and cloudy fears of our interlude had eclipsed the common perception of John Kennedy.

* * *

He called me the following week. I was pulled out of class and brought to the director's office, where the uncradled phone lay waiting. The director left and shut the door behind him.

"Are you on a secure line?" the president asked.

"Yes, there's no switchboard here, no extension. I'm alone with the door closed."

"Good. I wanted to ask a favor of you. Have you discussed our meeting with anyone?"

"Not in detail. I told a friend or two that we met and talked a little, but not what about. Except for J. D. Salinger."

He gave a short laugh.

"That's all right. That's fine. But about the rest of it, people or organizations I might have mentioned, I need for you to not tell anyone. To keep it, for now, in the strictest confidence."

"Yes, of course."

I had somehow had a sense of this already, which made his call somewhat redundant. He himself seemed relieved, however.

"Good, I appreciate it. If things go as they should, you'll understand. But say, have you gotten to *Franny and Zooey* yet?"

And that was that. A brief lighter exchange and I had spoken with Kennedy for the last time, at least in this life. I returned to my class in the language of ancient Rome, not yet aware that its intrigues persisted to our day.

* * *

A few months later, the month before congressional elections, the Cuban Missile Crisis occurred. While the outbreak of war seemed likely, the president held firm and the Soviets caved in. The cloud of fear lingered, however, and overshadowed the elections. The president's senatorial candidate lost in Illinois to the incumbent, while Mr. Nixon lost a challenge to the governor in California. People wanted to be safe. The following month, over fifty million dollars was paid to Castro to bring the Bay of Pigs veterans home for Christmas. It was a movement away from war, toward guarded coexistence.

I assumed that these events would delay Kennedy's action on the oil and arms profiteers. His brother Robert seemed to be assuming the greater role in domestic affairs, preparing major efforts against organized crime and the opponents of civil rights. But the resistance of Hoover and Governor Wallace forced the president to again assume leadership, relocate his focus to domestic issues. By July, after the integration issue had crested and somewhat receded, the overdue attention to oil and arms corruption could be paid. For the president, however, there were personal distractions surrounding the birth of his and Jackie's third child, who died within a few days. At the same time, Lee Harvey Oswald was getting to know the people in Texas who would take him to marksmanship training and get him the job in the book depository.

I sent a sympathy note after the baby's death, one of probably millions that were sent. I didn't expect a reply and didn't receive one. I was encouraged, though, by Kennedy's renewed interest in the lunar mission program, especially his invitation to Khrushchev to make it a joint American-Soviet project. While the premier rejected the idea, it was still a promise of distance from war and fear. I knew, of course, that there were those who would hold the invitation against the president, and for reasons material rather than ideological. Years later, Khrushchev's son revealed that the premier had changed his mind and decided to accept the invitation, but couldn't because Kennedy was killed the next week.

* * *

In the elections of 1964, the year following Kennedy's assassination, the president of the Zapata Offshore Company ran for senator from Texas. Running as a Republican, his defeat was probably sealed by the heavy vote against Goldwater in the presidential contest. Widespread obsession with the race for president caused other elections to receive little scrutiny, but I took a special interest when I saw that the Zapata head, George Bush, was a candidate. I learned he'd become a multimillionaire in the oil business over the past decade, having moved from New England for that apparent purpose. I mentioned him to an old law professor connected with my school, one who had been familiar with prominent people of the past.

"I believe the family branches from the upper classes in Britain," he said, "so in New England they were what they called 'blue bloods.' Wealthy investors and bankers, prosperous through the Depression, backed by the big financial houses in Britain."

"Would they have financed rearmament for the second world war?"

"Of course. It was their most lucrative opportunity at the time. Why do you ask?"

"I was thinking of Alger Hiss."

"Hiss? Oh, as FDR's watchdog on them. Yes, well, we know what that earned him."

"And now, with the current Bush's success at Zapata, could it be that same money at work?"

"Well, coming from generations of wealth, there's no way he started from scratch. Though it's convenient to say so in elections, of course."

"And the international connections?"

"Far-reaching and shadowy. Beyond Britain to continental Europe and South Africa. Secret operations under a parent company in Canada, Permindex, which also has branches in the U.S."

"Violence?"

He hesitated a moment.

"The lords of finance have a way of justifying what they do, however hateful it seems to outside observers. Their own prosperity is a sort of God-given destiny for them, with all the trappings of religion and nationalism. Their opponents, therefore, become embodiments of evil whose deaths are for the better and so needn't trouble their consciences."

"And the president last year? They would go that far?"

He gave me a teacher's look, tolerant of my naivete.

"Well, I suppose we should wait on the Warren Commission. But a dollar gets you ten they finish up for the elections!"

I was taken aback by his apparent cynicism. In fact, however, the Warren Report appeared in September and became most notable for what it left out or failed to pursue. It not only fostered endless speculation, but prevented additional truths about the killing from gaining credibility. I felt somewhat intimidated with my bit of knowledge on Kennedy's fate, and this feeling was no doubt shared by others who might have stepped forward in Garrison's and other investigations. Like them, however, I was left to observe an unfolding of events through the years in which Kennedy's foes played prominent parts.

* * *

I left the college-level seminary in 1966, disturbed over the Church's passivity toward the war in Vietnam. I thought they had misunderstood Kennedy's position and been biased toward the Diem regime, which had been overthrown the month Kennedy was killed. Lyndon Johnson did not seem concerned with limiting American involvement or the profits from it. His likely connections to other political and business figures from Texas inevitably came to mind. George Bush entered the House of Representatives the year I left the seminary, though he lost again in a Senate race in 1970. Garrison's prosecution of Clay Shaw occurred in the meantime, with evidence Shaw had run a branch of Permindex and known Lee Harvey Oswald. The British financial backers of Permindex had backed Bush's oil business, and his two Senate races as well. After the Watergate scandal, Bush toured the country giving speeches in defense of Nixon–the prosecutor of Hiss, the nemesis of Bush's father. Gerald Ford, a member of the Warren Commission, appointed Bush to head the CIA for a year to deal with the agency's past abuses. By the time the Democrats came in, he had supposedly done the job. It bespoke a prior acquaintance with the agency, though none was known. I recalled the warning of President Kennedy about a Zapata link to the CIA.

I reconciled with the Church after the Vietnam War and eventually joined a religious order, though not with any prospect for the priesthood. I didn't mind this because I felt the need for a lower-profile role, one in which I needn't be confrontational with what I knew and understood. I watched passively as a renewed swell of materialism overwhelmed the ideals of a generation. Like many others, however, I was jolted awake by the Iran-Contra Affair that became known late in 1986. While attention focused on the testimonies of Poindexter and North, I awaited news on the involvement of Vice President Bush. A fellow member of the National Security Council, he was more privy to covert operations than the sanguine, forgetful Reagan, and he'd attended key meetings. He was no doubt close to Casey, the CIA head who was implicated. Bush escaped scrutiny, however, perhaps due to Casey's death, with only passing interest from the media. I found that I wasn't surprised by this but was sourly disappointed. With Bush continuing to prosper and rise, my secret retained its significance and nourished my guilt.

* * *

During autumn of 1987, I was visited by an official from the Democratic Party. He came in the wake of the aggressive discrediting of Gary Hart, who had seemed a formidable opponent for Bush in the next presidential election. My visitor was about half a generation older than myself, well groomed and stylishly dressed. I had the impression I'd seen him before but couldn't recall where.

"We can't let that buzzard get in," he said. "I think you know why."

I'd been surprised enough by his visit, but this likely reference to my secret nearly froze me.

"I'm sorry about your man," I managed. "I was pulling for him. But surely one of the others can mount a strong campaign."

"Not a winning one. Not without some help."

I hesitated.

"Well, as you can see, I'm living a monastic life. The vow of poverty. The order itself doesn't make any political contributions."

"I wasn't thinking of money."

I attempted a puzzled look, but he went on.

"I understand you worked in the Yates campaign in '62, his Senate run. That you met with JFK when he went to Chicago for a fund-raiser."

"I don't recall it being a fund-raiser, just a reception.

And I wasn't a campaign worker. I was a guest of one of my teachers."

"But you spoke with Kennedy. In private."

"Who told you this?"

He paused, glancing at the floor.

"I'm sorry. It was in confidence."

"And if I told you what we spoke of, would that stay in confidence?"

"Well now, that wouldn't help us much, would it?"

"No."

"We'd have to cite our source, someone outside the party. It might call for a public appearance, an affidavit even. This is assuming, of course, something damaging to Bush."

"Something you know already?"

"Suspect, yes. But to help the vote we'll need Kennedy's own words to you. Then we and everyone else will truly know. A victory for us and for truth."

I had to smile. Maybe idealism wasn't dead, after all. But the thought of going public, and in the midst of a presidential campaign, made me squirm within.

"Can't you get this from someone else?"

"Intelligence agents aren't accessible to us, even if one were sympathetic. And Bobby's long gone."

"Ted?"

"Not in the loop. You caught the president in a rare moment. He must have doubted his own agents, wanted to leave a message in a bottle, so to speak."

And yet, he'd called the next week to withdraw the message. This was my out, though I needn't tell this visitor. I just said I wasn't ready, needed to think about it, and he took this surprisingly well. I assumed he'd be following up, but he simply left his card and didn't contact me again. I guessed there had been a change of strategy. Default candidate Dukakis showed early strength, but then wilted under Bush commercials that distorted his record as governor. My worst fear for America had come true, and I accepted the rigors of monastic life as expiation for my guilt.

* * *

I wasn't surprised when Bush, without Congressional approval, authorized the invasion of Panama in 1989. It deflected attention from his poor performance as president, as well as continuing the string of military adventures begun under Reagan. It thus reinforced the demands of Cheney, the Secretary of Defense, for continued high military spending despite the decline of communism. Of course, the Gulf War in 1991 served these purposes much better by virtue of its larger scale, and it won back control of the region's oil for Western companies and financiers. OPEC's as well as Hussein's power was reduced, but at a terrible cost to the civilians of Iraq.

I was worried during this time about an Iraqi woman I had known while a secular student. She had returned to Iraq right after graduating and was part of the small Christian community in Baghdad. The bombing in that city was clearly directed at its infrastructure, especially its electricity and water supply, rather than at military targets. Young children were especially vulnerable to the resulting health hazards, and hundreds of thousands of them died. On thinking of my friend, I estimated that any children she had would be in their teens, so their chances were better. But I wondered how she would handle their feelings toward the Americans who wrought the destruction, the glib generals and chortling politicians talking about "collateral damage." It was hard to imagine the moral bankruptcy that enabled men to cause such things, and simply to sustain the life of wealth to which they were accustomed.

The United Nations and Congress had considered economic sanctions against Iraq, and defense of Saudi Arabia against

Iraqi forces in Kuwait. For Bush, however, nothing short of offensive war would do. He amassed twice the troops he had originally requested, then ordered the attack at his earliest opportunity. This eagerness to involve the U.S. in warfare persisted even when he was defeated in the next election. Bush used his closing weeks in office to mire our country in the factional fighting in Somalia, creating an unnecessary handicap for the new administration.

* * *

Some of the monks here were amused by the farcical 2000 election, and I could appreciate this. It was a harmless diversion from monastic life and made them easier to live with. But for me, the drawn-out accession of another George Bush was a long nightmare, and so was the return of Cheney. He had spent the intervening years reaping financial rewards from the revolving door between the military and industry. In addition to joining several boards of directors, Cheney became the CEO of Haliburton, a company that had helped finance Permindex. He arranged for Haliburton to merge with Dresser Industries, creating the world's largest oil-drilling services company.

In the early months of his term, it appeared that the younger George Bush's limitations might actually limit the damage he would do. With the terrible attacks of September 11, however, a situation arose in which a leader could gain approval without the benefit of higher mental or expressive abilities. Responding to public anger, Bush presented the great crime as a basis for war before the surviving suspects were even identified. Any chance for international police action, for careful investigation and prosecution, was out the window. Instead there was the massive bombing of Afghanistan, in which thousands of non-suspects were killed and yet the chief suspects escaped. This crudeness of approach, moreover, has become the younger Bush's basic technique. His actions and demands, however questionable, are parts of his war on terrorism, so to question them is deemed unpatriotic. The finer points of issues needn't be dealt with.

As the proponents for war clamor to attack Iraq again, I think once more about my friend there. Any sons she had are now mature adults, probably expected to serve in the army. They've no doubt been influenced by her quiet nature, intelligence, and Christian values, as I'm sure the daughter has. Yet now they must defend their country against a massive and merciless U.S. invasion, said to be a war on terrorism. I find it incredible how few of my countrymen realize that, for each generation of a people we attack, a younger generation sees the pain and humiliation, which plants a seed of hatred that can blossom into revenge.

It has become known that Bush and his advisors had advance information on the attacks, but did not respond. His few public critics generously ascribe this to incompetence. And yet these terrible events, including the violence in Afghanistan, have resulted in considerable gains for Bush and the financial interests he represents. Afghanistan has vast untapped resources and an oil pipeline route that are now open to exploitation. These same interests would collect from a crushing of Iraq, gaining complete and lasting control of the oil industry. The warfare conducted in these and other places reaps enormous profits for the arms industry, as well as the financiers behind it. Some of the most prominent belong to the Carlyle Group, a private military investment company that includes the elder George Bush.

I know, as I walk the edge of our grounds under myriad stars, that I share in the responsibility for all that has happened. I was personally warned of it by John Kennedy, yet I did nothing. But I'm hopeful that, through a principle suggested by those distant stars, the precise truth will someday be known. Just as we see those points of light as they existed millions of years ago, so a device shot far enough into space could see all that has happened in these recent decades. The conspirators will then be identified, the task that was mine accomplished.

(End of Thomas's narrative.)

3.

Irose with the sun next morning, having slept well, surprisingly so for a single night in a strange room. No one was about when I went downstairs, so I took the liberty of starting coffee in the kitchen. Sandra came in as I was listening for birds above the coffee bubbling. There were none, however, so she was my assurance that life goes on after even the greatest losses.

"Like some breakfast?" she asked.

"Maybe just some toast, and your company."

"We have some almost-fresh muffins."

"Fine."

"Have a seat."

Conversation was sparse as we sat there at the table. Business had been attended to, my departure was imminent, there was no clear need for further communication. From her glances during the gaps, however, I knew something was on her mind. It could only be the document. I had to say something, I thought.

"I opened the envelope last night."

She looked at me and waited.

"It was something Thomas wrote. Seventeen pages, typed."

"Does it affect me or Natalya, or the house?"

"No. It's about things from way back, mostly before you knew him. Nothing about here."

Sandra relaxed a bit. She glanced toward the gathering sunlight at the kitchen window.

"I suppose you can't tell me much more. For your eyes only and all."

"Well, maybe another time. I have to sort some things out, understand them better. And there might be things for me to do."

She nodded. I soon rose and went to collect my things.

I drove the same roads on my return trip, but they somehow looked different to me with my greater knowledge of Thomas. His conflicts, his angst, served to expand his character as a friend, drinking companion, confidant. And then there was Natalya, the further option for Mr. R_____ should he need another heir against the Order. It had been an informative visit for me and I felt appreciative. At this stage of my life, personal awareness superseded financial considerations, though I'd try to research those old baseball cards.

First, however, there was the question of the manuscript. What had been Thomas's intention in leaving it to me? He'd clearly had confidence in me, marking it for my eyes only, while wanting Sandra and Natalya disconnected from it, thus shielding them from attention. The attention would come from outsiders, reacting to the narrative appearing in a publication. This was, I thought, what Thomas at some level wanted: dissemination. It was inconceivable to me that I should just read his paper and lock it away, or destroy it. I was to make a judgment and act on it. Thomas had wanted some things known.

I took some time to reflect, as is my wont, and then followed a simple plan. I made eight copies of the manuscript, bought some large envelopes, and sent the packets to six large city newspapers and two weeklies. I included a brief letter explaining the posthumous nature of the submission. This was the best I thought I could do. I then settled in to wait, knowing a response would take time if in fact one ever came.

When I say "settled in," I mean it in a rather strong sense. I'd retired early and for a number of years had been living alone. I'd tried to approximate the bachelor years of my youth but of course that was impossible. Mine was an essentially senior routine: reading after breakfast, having long casual walks, searching for nuggets of meaning in the residual culture. I used to habitually browse in bookstores, but they had mostly disappeared. So instead I studied buildings, their architecture, the presence or lack of taste. I was especially drawn to churches, their possible appeal to one's spiritual sensibility. I had long abandoned religious practice, however, so I also felt a sense of estrangement. It was in this way, this difference, that I felt the most separate from Thomas, whose faith superseded even his closest personal ties.

There eventually came a response to the packets I'd sent out. It was from the San Francisco paper, thanking me for my submission and saying they would like to publish it but unfortunately could not. It did not elaborate, though it was not a form letter and was signed by one of the editors. It seemed I was supposed to understand something, some legality or limitation of newspapers. After more time passed with no further response, I decided to call one of the weeklies, a local one circulated for free, to find out what the problem was. I had to leave a message and await a call back, which came a while later from a young assistant editor.

"The thing is," he said, "it's mostly unverifiable. What's offered as new information, I mean. The historical stuff is okay, the reasoning pretty good. But on those conversations, with the president and others, we only have his word they took place, and on what was said."

"I knew the author a long time. I'm sure he wouldn't fabricate."

"Yes, I can respect that. But on anything we get we have to check the facts before we publish. And that's not entirely possible in this case."

"So, there's no way it could be published then?"

The editor sighed.

"Well, I suppose you could try the academic world. Some professor doing research might use it, at least as a footnote. Or you could present it as fact-based fiction, like the movie *JFK*."

Our conversation soon ended, I thanking the editor and he glad to be done with me. I was left with no worthwhile move to make. I was too old, I thought, to become an advocate, "blogging" and calling in to TV and radio shows. And I wasn't sure of Thomas's intent in that regard, how far he'd wish me to go. There were still Sandra and Natalya to think about. And then, like it or not, I had to consider Thomas's credibility. Despite my defense of him to the editor, Thomas had sometimes been a story teller, a wry joker. I couldn't rule out that influence on the material at hand. Material which, at best, could only become a footnote in some esoteric journal.

I returned to the cigar box, the other part of Thomas's legacy to me. The baseball cards, I observed, would have greater value in society than Thomas's writing, and the life behind it. Adulation of pro athletes trumped critical revelations. Then there were the gears he'd collected, so meaningless lying in the box. And yet they'd held some truth for him, some appeal. Some sort of attraction. Perhaps some mystery was necessary in Thomas, unknown facets like his life with Sandra and Natalya. Necessary to make him who he was.

I decided to take a walk.

It was a pleasant day, quiet in my apartment complex and the neighborhood beyond. I came to a small park and sat down on a bench. There was no one else in sight, though cars were parked by the houses and at a school nearby. I reflected that this could be my afterlife, this well-tamed emptiness. Some birds I hadn't noticed edged toward me along the ground. They were accustomed to being fed here, I thought, but I had nothing to offer them. Nothing, nothingness. Was it all that I'd had to offer *anyone*? Compared to Thomas, at least, and he had been rejected, relegated to oblivion. Well, then maybe I should have no regrets. I was the lesser of us two and could have gotten no further than he, anyway.

Then there was the question of why. What did it matter how you succeeded in society, in the world? But I was answered by my distant past, a concern for quality in living, for adhering to an ideal spiritual standard, that haunting presence. Life was to be lived as well as possible, in all ways, thus justifying one's birth.

I could get up from the bench, I thought, walk back the way I'd come to a restaurant near my apartment. I could have a drink or two in Thomas's memory, let things go at that. But I didn't move yet. I decided to linger awhile, see if anything more came to me that I'd forgotten.

ACCELERATED MOVEMENT

1.

The drive to Lansing was uneventful, allowing Dr. Patmos to mull his feelings. Leaving mistress and wife was like stepping out of water, he thought, one foot from warm and the other from cold. He smiled to himself, smugly as he might with his students. He'd like to share that with Shakler, whom he'd see on this trip, but he knew the Canadian wouldn't react. He'd glance sideways toward nothing in particular, then talk immediately about business, seemingly rude. It wasn't his fault, Patmos thought; he'd been through a lot, had given a lot up.

Shakler was not a native Canadian. He'd moved there to avoid the draft for the Vietnam War. Though covered by the general pardon that came later, he never moved back. He worked at a series of mundane jobs and then went into business for himself. As far as Patmos knew, Shakler had never married. He wouldn't discuss his personal involvements, social or political, except for the Shortfall Club and its secret inner group. It seemed Shakler had been watching from afar for a very long time, inwardly analyzing the history of his native country, relating it to his fate and assigning responsibility. He lived now with mature awareness, unfazed by emotionalism or ideologies. He wasn't looking to get rich, or to gain love or power, but Patmos sensed he had a goal that was a positive need, perhaps for resolution. The professor felt a flicker of fear when he talked with Shakler.

They met at Dirtbag's Tavern, equidistant from the

university and the government buildings. Shakler was waiting for him, seated casually at a table with a stein of beer in front of him. He acknowledged Patmos with a thin smile, a gentler version of his potent stare. Patmos ordered a beer.

"Had lunch?" Shakler inquired.

"No."

"We'll order sandwiches when she gets back."

He pulled a menu off the condiment holder and pushed it at Patmos.

"I already checked it. The brisket sounds good."

Patmos glanced at the menu and tucked it back. He trusted Shakler's judgment, enjoyed the break from having to use his own. The waitress came and they ordered their sandwiches.

"So," said Shakler, "how are we doing at the Shortfall Club?"

"No new decisions. Members mostly looking for the discounts. Tax return's still delinquent. They don't want to accept Mr. Singh's accounting."

Shakler chuckled, low and confidential.

"I don't blame them."

His smile faded and he glanced slowly around the room.

"And the brothers?" he asked.

"We have a new one, apparently. I'll meet him Thursday at the conclave. He might be just what we wanted–a cooler type, tenacious–to balance out the others."

"What's his name?"

"Byron Horne. Dr. Lamont did the full check on him. He's been drifting quite a while. Never satisfied, smart, the classic loner looking for a cause."

Shakler stared with watery gray eyes.

"Sounds good. As long as he's solid, we'll move at once on the next project."

Patmos was taken aback. Their previous project, the burning of a municipal garage, had been practice for something more significant. He hadn't expected it this soon, however. They'd barely settled on who was in their operating group.

"The brothers, they want a name to operate under. They're suggesting 'Talons of the Phoenix.'"

Shakler looked away, reflecting.

"Sounds kind of video-game. I'd have opted for something more subtle, sophisticated. But the point is to be effective. If it helps them do the work, let them have the name they want. 'Talons' it is."

The waitress brought their sandwiches. They ate for a while, but the unresolved question of the new project hung between them. Though the tension surrounding the first project was still fresh in his mind, Patmos wanted to show solidarity. So he returned to the subject himself, asking Shakler what he was planning.

"Well, first of all, let's be clear that we want to go ahead. We can minimize the risks, but there can still be unintended results. They get more likely as we go up the ladder. Are you ready to accept that? Some problems as we pursue our goals?"

"Of course," Patmos replied.

The promptness of his answer seemed to surprise Shakler. But for Patmos the challenge had brought his mistress to mind, as if *she* were asking the question, testing him as her lover.

"All right, then," Shakler continued. He glanced around and spoke softly. "This is still developmental, but we want to step up to explosives and a more substantial target. Government, of course."

"Still the no-casualty rule?"

"Absolutely. We're not killers, unlike them. That has to be understood, has to be our message."

"Agreed. And the target, this more substantial one?"

"A rest stop on one of the interstates."

Patmos took a moment to absorb this, verify that Shakler was serious. But then, he was always serious. He was dead set on it, in fact. It was the product of many years of lonely deliberation. So there was no reason to laugh, or even to question very far.

"It would have to be empty, not in use. Is one of them closed?"

"I don't know. But it doesn't matter because we're going for one that's business as usual. Except we'll hit it when there's no one inside. Middle of the night, early morning."

"But the traffic going by is constant. There's no way to be sure—"

"That's where your new guy comes in, the new 'Talon.' We need someone with ice in his veins sitting right in front of the facility, after it's been rigged, to give the word on when to detonate."

"The bombers are somewhere else?"

"They're at the rest stop on the other side of the interstate, for traffic going the other way. They detonate by remote control."

"What about Byron, sitting right in front?"

"He gets ten seconds after giving the word. So he has to have his motor running and facing the ramp when he gives the go."

"That's cutting it pretty close."

"Has to be, so no one goes inside after he leaves."

"Understood. But can't they just watch through binoculars for when it's clear?"

"Too chancy. There's trees, traffic in the way. And we don't know what the weather will be like. Plus, we want the option of looking inside in case any doubt arises."

Patmos looked away, visualizing the scene. He would have to sell this to the Talons at their conclave. Some would be eager to proceed, but one or two might have doubts, as he himself vaguely did.

"What about expertise?"

"Well, on the programming we have Dr. Lamont, plus Collins with his Air Force training. You yourself can determine the charge we need. Let The Postman get the explosives through his old contacts. Use as many lookouts as possible during the rigging, so we can work calmly, safely."

"How many charges?"

"That's up to you. But of course, we *do* want to send a message. We can't have them thinking it was just an accident, fireworks or something."

"Agreed."

They talked awhile about parts, Shakler saying he could bring them in himself if necessary. But Patmos knew he could get what they needed from the labs at the university, so it seemed they were ready to go ahead. They finished their lunch and Shakler suggested they have a stroll.

"There are the public gardens nearby," he said. "Professional interest."

As they walked, Shakler seemed aloof from his surroundings, his long legs striding at a relaxed pace. He gazed into the farthest distance, expressionless. The traffic beside them was heavy and noisy.

"Unlimited production of cars, other vehicles," Shakler said. "Funny we haven't reached permanent gridlock."

"Well," said Patmos, "there's planned obsolescence."

Shakler laughed.

"Our savior. Obsolescence as value. Tells you who's in charge, doesn't it?"

"Yes, unfortunately."

"The bottom-liners. Sitting at the top with society all arranged for them. White House on down."

"People buy into it, though. The products, the wars. Agree with the corporate line or you're not patriotic. Life is now a string of banal, short-term goals for which people give up their dignity, and other people's. Obey the boss, adore the flag, kill the designated enemy."

"An old problem, though, Vietnam and before. The 'Greatest

Generation,' greatest at needing enemies and sending young guys to kill or be killed. They had to keep feeling like heroes after Hitler was gone, no matter how much death and ruin they caused."

"Well, there was no real culture to fall back on. What do we have in comparison with the old cultures of Europe and Asia? Their achievements in art, literature, and science over the ages? We make the most bombs, justify their use on TV, treat them as toys in video games. That's our culture."

"Yeah," said Shakler. "That's why it's fair game."

They came to the gardens, an oasis of vegetation amid the bustle of the state capital. Patmos waited respectfully as Shakler examined plants, then sat with him on a bench. Staff and clients from the government buildings walked past them.

"So, here we are," said Patmos, "relaxing with the two-party system."

"Well, why not? Doesn't it belong in the Shortfall Club?"

"Certainly. If only more people could see it–"

"They won't as long as they see two parties, instead of the *one* that's really there."

"That single corporate agenda, rumbling along unopposed. The smokescreen of red herring issues."

"The Republicans are best at that. But I blame the Democrats more. The constant selling out, being absorbed into the imperial program."

"Yet they still give the illusion of representing the masses, thus cutting off any third-party momentum."

"The masses, yeah. With their fears and bigotry ready to be exploited by politicians. The media, too. Return the plan for empire to another term."

"Well, the media is corporate turf. Progressives are shut out and, with the failure of the Democrats, disenfranchised."

Shakler looked in his eyes.

"And, at the core?"

"The core?"

"The core of the progressives."

"Oh. Well, alienated I suppose."

Shakler looked back to the bureaucrats. Patmos sensed an icy confidence building.

"There are some smart people in those movements," Shakler said, "but it isn't enough just to be right. You also have to make an impact. Do some damage. The big boys just laugh at demonstrations, petitions, et cetera."

"As the old tycoons laughed at the early unions. They would tolerate no rules in amassing their wealth."

"Those bastards. They even wanted colonies, didn't they? The Spanish-American War?"

"A set-up, yes. And now we've come full circle. The mentality is back in force. Today some Arab land, tomorrow the world."

"Which is where *we* come in."

"Sabotage."

"Yeah," Shakler smiled, "for a start."

2.

As he stood at his living-room window, Shakler could view the skylines of both Windsor and Detroit, the twin edges of his dual citizenship. Behind him, the afternoon sun stretched his shadow, broad-shouldered but gaunt, through the spacious living room. A huge reproduction of Modigliani's mistress, by Rudomine, graced the wall above the main couch. This was a source of irritation for Claudine, who was visiting that day from Montreal, since she felt it distracted from political discussion. But Shakler had lost his taste for the abstract, was interested now only in the literal, cutting through the chaff. Too many rules or ideals were a hindrance to success, the achievement of your vital goals.

The stare of Shakler's watery gray eyes was disarming to most people. He kept his wavy, whitish hair cut short to lessen the effect, but he wasn't really sorry that he bothered people. It was a convenient preemptive strike, after all–a warning not to pull anything on him. They were dealing with an unknown quantity in him, perhaps a man of violence.

Going to his computer, Shakler accessed the site of the Shortfall Club, a social organization for losers that recruited via the Internet. It contained a secret inner circle of militants, the Talons of the Phoenix. While Shakler had no official connection to them, the Talons were available to follow his directives. His link was Dr. Patmos, president of the Shortfall Club and supposed head of the Talons, as well as a physics professor in Michigan. Shakler had become the professor's confidant during a political campaign–third-party futility–and now supplied the planning for a more effective effort. He now opened the file on the Shortfall Club membership, the ersatz talent pool for recruiting Talons.

While Shakler had a legitimate landscaping business, there was no sign of it in the apartment. He left it entirely at his facility in a nearby commercial zone, thus maintaining total control of his personal environment. The business was a convenient cover, he thought, giving him an acceptable shell in Canadian society. He'd trained for it working for someone else, gaining an extensive knowledge of decorative stone and perennials.

Claudine arrived while he was at the computer. She took a seat beneath Modigliani's mistress while Shakler eased back in his recliner. He'd taken a Cuban cigar from a nearby humidor and proceeded to light up.

"Do you really enjoy those?" Claudine asked. "Or are you making a statement?"

"Enjoy? It's for the experience. I'm not a leftist. I'm a classicist."

"No, you're not."

"Well, except with you."

Claudine smiled, only a small change in her face. She had strong features, with deep-set eyes amid olive complexion. Her brown hair was full and wavy. Two decades younger than Shakler, she was big-boned but had no excess weight.

"You look like an old robber baron," she said.

"A laissez-faire? Wedded to the British banking houses? Bush's relatives?"

She laughed.

"That would make you a Bush."

Shakler looked away from her, toward a window.

"Old Prescott, playing both sides for World War II. Financed the arms buildup for Germany, among others. Then he fattened up as a Cold War senator, teaching George the ropes. Those same British banks financed George the First's campaigns. Always money and war, war and money–colonies along the way."

"And the CIA."

"Ah yes, protecting national security by making enemies around the world."

"All for freedom."

"Yeah, freedom–the freedom of the banking class via Big Oil and the war industries. Honored with songs before every ball game."

"Easy now, Shakler. You're on the good side of the border."

He looked at her lazily with his long, thin smile, eyes half closed.

"You *make* it good," he said.

Claudine smiled again, but with a stir in her shoulders. Shakler took note and put out his cigar. It was time for some business.

"I take it," he said, "there's news from the guild."

Claudine hesitated.

"Yes, they were impressed. The total destruction, everyone escaping–it was quite efficient for a new group."

"Why do I get the feeling this is a good and bad news thing?"

'Well, after all, Shakler, bombing a toilet stop along a highway! There's a question of significance. If they're going to help you, they want to feel it's worthwhile."

"Okay, I get the picture. Actually, it was an expensive rest area with all major systems, a real problem to replace under a strained state budget. But why quibble? Of *course* we'll be going for bigger things. This gig was just to develop the group."

"Sort of a training run? An exercise?"

"Exactly."

She nodded, appraising now.

"So when does training day phase into hitting high-priority targets?"

"Real soon, maybe next time out. We need to recruit a few more operatives, but we've got a tested, efficient core now. You yourself said they did well."

Claudine shrugged.

"It's a step up from burning the bus garage."

They shared a laugh.

"That was suggested by one of the Talons. An inner-city guy."

"They'll laugh about it themselves as they move on."

"I'm sure."

"Are you hungry yet? I didn't stop for lunch."

They decided to walk to Beau Jim's, a quiet restaurant on the way to the nightclub strip. The evening crowd was not yet gathering, so they got in easily without a reservation. Shakler ordered fillet of sole, which came lightly nestled on Boston lettuce, while Claudine had a petite filet mignon. She chewed it with obvious relish.

"You know, Shakler, another thing came up in the guild. The 'no casualties' dictate that you give your operatives. I mean, insisting on property damage only is ultimately going to limit your effectiveness."

Shakler gave her his stare, disarming to most people. Claudine had long since adjusted to it, however.

"The basic appeal of our work," he said, "is that we take a higher moral ground than our adversaries. That's how we recruit people. Why should they join if we ourselves seem morally questionable?"

"I understand, but I'm not talking about recruitment. I'm talking about down the road, as your projects progress. Maybe you should loosen the shackles a bit. After all, if the other side senses your limits, they could write you off as just some latter-day hippie, or guru. Purely symbolic, and no threat to them personally."

Shakler tried the smile.

"Well, we know that's not true."

"Yes, but *they* don't. That's the point."

"So then, we're talking bodily harm? That's the price for support from the guild?"

"Not harm in the gratuitous sense. You know I'd never support something like that. But when it comes to selected targets, individuals–well, they think you should be more flexible."

Flexible, Shakler thought–his own approach being sprung against him. Claudine was learning, all right.

"Are you having dessert?" he asked.

"Of course!"

After they left Beau Jim's, they decided to take a walk through the nightclub strip. It was starting to gain momentum for Saturday night. Shakler soon grew tense and took long strides, making Claudine step quickly to keep up.

"Tell you what," he said. "Time's starting to run short for me. 'Movements' as such don't have much meaning–I mean *promise*, for results in my lifetime. Direct action, yes. Drastic moves to guarantee results. That's our business, right? So I'm willing, you know, to step things up like you and the guild say. I'm agreeable."

They stopped at a quiet corner. Small trees were planted in squares of earth amid the cement. Shakler's professional eye judged the workmanship. Claudine smoothed her hair in the chill wind that had risen.

"So *how* willing are you, Shakler? Can we say that the ban on casualties is off?"

"I have an idea," Shakler replied, "something that will tie in with my plan for multiple strikes in our next project. Two venues–one government target and one corporate, thus making transition to our main enemy. Well, I'll keep that much. But I'll drop the ban on casualties and even make fatalities our goal–only they won't be human!"

Claudine continued to push her hair back in the wind, conditioned against surprise at anything Shakler might say.

"We'll go after animals they own. Expensive pets, prize livestock and such. Time the two strikes so there's no doubt about their connection."

"The owners being two prominent figures."

"Right. Maybe cabinet level, CEO, CFO, COO–"

Claudine looked away, let her hair fly.

"It beats blowing up toilets," she said.

They returned to Shakler's apartment.

"There's another possibility," Claudine said when they arrived.

"Oh?"

"It involves the Earth Freedom Force."

"Destroyers of rustic condos and gas-hog vehicles?"

"Well, this is a rogue cell, or cluster. More chutzpah than the EFF in general. They've been known to harass, intimidate, even one brief kidnapping. Someone in the guild has contact with them."

"Where do they operate?"

"Alberta and B.C. on our side, and the states down to Salt Lake, where your guy can meet with them."

"They cover a big area."

"But not much population. They're looking to expand their impact, sort of like you. Get beyond the regional and explode some issues nationally. They won't insist on staying with the environment."

Shakler lit his partial cigar, savored this offer of new power, unexpected progress.

"Do you have someone you can send to Salt Lake?" Claudine asked. "Clean, and low visibility?"

"Uh-huh, this young guy we just moved up. Has a master's and he's a marksman, too. Learned it hunting, no military. His name is Emmett."

"So shall I set it up?"

"Yeah, go ahead."

"Okay. And you're welcome."

Shakler smiled as he started to puff.

"I don't ever take you for granted, Claudine."

She eyed him through the smoke. Business, Shakler thought, is close to finishing for the day.

"I've got plenty of wine," he said. "Like a booster?"

"That would be nice."

They sipped the red wine without saying much, holding up their glasses to view the color. Claudine smiled coyly after a while, but it wasn't yet the bedroom look. She was still holding back.

"Can you use a SAM?" she asked.

"A *what*?"

"Surface-to-air missile. For when you really get serious, as we know you will."

Shakler started to smile, but of course she wasn't kidding. This wasn't just Claudine speaking; it was the guild.

"Getting a bit ahead of ourselves, aren't we?"

"If you want to score big, you'll need the right equipment. We could slip it into a machinery shipment, or you could take it over with your usual junk."

"Junk? Oh, you mean the noble tools of my profession."

Claudine was silent. Maybe it wasn't all that crazy, he thought, just seemed so to his staid methodology. While flexible, he'd been prone to strong caution.

"Can they afford to give one up? Surely a SAM was on their own wish lists."

"Well, there's something heavier on the way." She hesitated, then: "A mini-nuke."

"Come on."

"They got access to a prototype from a British research intern. The hot stuff they pick up in Ukraine."

"Still for the highest bidder, hey?"

"Actually, it's rather cheap now."

Shakler swirled wine in his glass, letting the news sink in. Perhaps he'd been moving too slowly.

"I'll take the SAM," he said. "And thank you, Claudine."

She smiled without replying. Her work is done, Shakler thought, so she can relax. But was not her work also his? This help they were giving him, as they gave it to others, was part of an effort to establish a wide pattern of actions. The eventual effect of these mounting actions would be to force change–perhaps collapse–of the overriding order that gripped the planet. As the Soviet Union had fallen, and the colonial empires before them, so would corporate hegemony. It was a world-wide problem, exploiting peoples and resources. He and those like him were the antidote.

3.

Emmett, with his clean-cut good looks, worked as a counselor in his local school system. His wife, Kirsten, had been a teacher until the birth of their daughter the previous year. Kirsten knew about the Shortfall Club and accepted it as connected to Emmett's work. She did *not* know of his involvement with the Talons for Earth Freedom, and would have been shocked to learn of it. Her husband was educated and non-violent, while the Talons employed brutal force in their campaign against corporate power. Emmett couldn't reveal his secret role to Kirsten because his purpose was to protect her and their daughter, both from the corruption in society and the consequences of his actions. He'd committed his life to the Talons' success, but those close to him mustn't suffer for it.

Though he was paid fairly for his work, Emmett was aware of others in society who received much more for less effort, less learning, less caring about their fellow man. He'd noted the tenacity of "old money," as well as the legacies of ruthless "entrepreneurs" and their offspring. High-placed bankers and corporate officers, financiers, and others formed a society within the society, one that stretched its tentacles internationally. Their politicians presented stubborn wrongness as strength, rational compromise as weakness. A crude appeal to nationalism would thus be used to justify a war, all the time serving the corporate and related agendas. The public could be distracted with stock issues such as abortion and gun control, or lulled to sleep through corporate control of media and culture.

Even among family and friends, Emmett found a dimming awareness of the corporate designs on health care, social security, and the environment. Beyond his fragile circle lay the confused mass of society, with its endless violence, decay, and self-abasement. The two-party system, America's model for the world, had been co-opted by corporate power. Fringe groups on the left and right provided impotent opposition, serving only to legitimize the existing monopoly. No, beyond a few friends and his modest income, there was no supportive network for Emmett's family. This was what he saw and resented, what he chose to fight against in the Talons for Earth Freedom.

* * *

The van containing four men and a surface-to-air missile had proceeded smoothly from Ohio to Connecticut. It was somewhat cramped in the back, where the SAM components were concealed among rugs and computer boxes, but the driver and front passenger were entirely comfortable. The men were members of the Talons for Earth Freedom, an alliance of social militant groups. Until recently, the occupants of the van had been Talons of the Phoenix, but their leadership had forged an alliance with a rogue cluster within the Earth Freedom Force, which was environmental in focus. The new organization would continue to oppose corporate control of society and government, as the Phoenix group had done, but with a global perspective and statements of responsibility for their actions.

Throughout the current trip, the van's front passenger seat had been occupied by Dr. Lamont. He was dressed in "office casual," his sandy hair and goatee fresh from the styling shop. He'd normally supervise an attack from afar, but for this one he'd be on-site. It was their first project under the new name and they were using equipment from backers in Canada. Extra effort must be made to retain the confidence of the other groups. If all went well, the Talons for Earth Freedom would surge in stature and have no trouble gaining support, both in dollars and in bodies.

The driving had been shared by Byron, the newest member on the trip, and Emmett, who had represented the Phoenix group at the alliance meeting. Emmett was actually the youngest in the van, his light brown hair cut clean, while Byron was shaggy with touches of gray. The fourth member of the team, The Postman, was in back with the missile for the duration of the trip. He gazed out from his tousled dark curls and tinted glasses. While sometimes prone to anxiety, he'd shown a calm, purposeful demeanor during this trip. He'd be the one shouldering the SAM when launch time came.

"Of course," Dr. Lamont was saying, "it isn't the *concept* of incorporation we oppose. We don't want people to get *that* idea. In theory, the corporation is a neutral thing, established and accepted for two or three centuries. Nobody's looking to turn all businesses into mom-and-pop stores, including us."

"Then there's the non-business corporations," said Emmett.

"Right. Charities, schools, cities and towns. If we talk about dismantling *everything*, we become ideological wackos."

"Communists maybe," said The Postman.

"More like nihilists," Lamont continued. "They wouldn't have any ideology to link us with. We'd be seen as backward–social Luddites, Druids–the direct opposite of what we are: progressive."

"So," said Byron behind the wheel, "we want people to know it's just *certain* corporations we oppose." He glanced at Lamont for confirmation.

"The *abuse* of incorporation, yes. Its use to consolidate power for nefarious purposes. Both specific instances and repeated patterns."

"With an eye, maybe," said Emmett, "toward world corporate hegemony."

Dr. Lamont turned in his seat and smiled.

"You're getting ahead of me, son. But yeah, there's the big picture. The multinationals, their control of governments, whole regions of the world, war and peace."

"The wars," said The Postman. "They show themselves in the wars."

"They try not to. But yes, they're usually there."

"So how do we get the word out, let people know we ain't wackos, just fighting these takeover guys?"

"Well," said Lamont, "to an extent our actions speak for themselves. But I guess we're about to supplement those messages. Right, Emmett?"

He and The Postman eyed their comrade expectantly.

"Yes," he answered, "it came out of the alliance. We're going to claim responsibility for our actions. That is, the TEF will. Our friends out west will do the claiming on this one."

"No kidding," sneered The Postman. "We do the work and they take the credit."

"The point is," said Dr. Lamont, "they *are* us. We're all one group, so they're taking credit for us, too."

"So what they gonna do? Make calls, send letters to editors?"

"Maybe," Emmett replied, "but for sure they'll spread it around the Internet. That's their specialty. The group they broke from was doing it right along."

"Can't a claim like that be traced?" asked Byron.

"Not the way they do it. Any investigation leads to a dead end, a raid on an empty room."

"I can respect that," said Dr. Lamont. "And we'll be pooling resources with them, data bases and such. Actually, they provided some info for the present job."

He looked out the window when no one answered. The reality of the western group had settled into the van, but there was also the reality of the project itself, growing more and more vivid as they neared their destination. It was a watershed for the Talons, since none of their previous actions had claimed a human life. And for Emmett it was something more, a personal crisis. His growing role within the Talons, as a leader and perhaps planner, was conflicting with an old commitment to respect life in all its forms. He wanted to achieve the Talons' aims, to save future societies from corporate domination and abuse, but deep within he didn't want to kill. He'd gone hunting with his father but never really liked it, and that was only animals.

The target of the operation was Dick Hanlon, a news spinner who blathered for an hour each night in prime time. He set the tone for other shows on the network, promoting crude politics with a corporate agenda behind it. Any challenge to this power structure, its culture of nationalism and religiosity, he reviled. It wouldn't have been bad if he'd simply expressed his views; they were expressed by many others, anyway. But he insisted, echoing the claim of the network, that his treatment of the news was fair and balanced. To support this claim, he'd sometimes host the holder of an opposing view, whom he would then interrupt and shout down at will. It was this tendency to manipulate the news, by Hanlon and the others, that had to be taught a lesson.

"Turnoff for Newbridge coming up," said The Postman.

"Got it," Byron acknowledged.

"We'll be at a local-brand motel," said Dr. Lamont. "No budget-chain place was close enough. If they get conversational, we're computer techies doing an installation."

The Postman grunted.

"So when do we case for the strike?"

"Tomorrow morning, very early. We have to drive a ways. We'll hang on the point and watch his copter pass. It'd be better if we didn't show the SAM yet."

"That's okay. I know how to handle it."

"We'll do just one run-through?" asked Emmett.

"One is plenty," said Lamont. "He's very precise in his schedule, obsessive-compulsive. We have our police and coast guard info, so we mostly just want to get a feel for the place."

They arrived in Newbridge and Byron cruised the streets around the Bluebird Motel. Dr. Lamont and The Postman got out at a seafood restaurant, where they'd have dinner. Byron and Emmett proceeded to the motel, where they'd check in and have a pizza delivered. Lamont and The Postman would check in separately, thus making the Talons less conspicuous as a group.

"So far, so good," said Emmett in the room.

"Yeah," Byron answered, "but this place is kind of hokey, don't you think?"

"You mean that manager living here, her place right behind the desk?"

"Yeah, and that business they have in back, the trailers and all."

Emmett shrugged.

"It's not neat and impersonal like we're used to, but we can adjust. Avoid them till checkout. Maybe just leave the keys in the room. No personal contact."

Byron nodded as he unpacked his things. They weren't quite in sync with each other, Emmett thought, despite their shared field of work, the social services. It disappointed him. Maybe his greater role in the Talons had something to do with it.

"Want me to call for the pizza?" Byron asked.

"Sure. Just so you get some vegetables on it."

Nothing like food to bring people together, Emmett considered. Although, whatever their perspectives, they were most strongly linked by their dedication to the Talons. That's what he had to remember. Interpersonal differences, just like his long-held personal values, had to be set aside so the Talons could triumph. He felt confident Byron would agree.

"I want to share something with you, Byron," he said over his third slice of pizza.

"Besides the room and the pizza? And the driving? The Postman might call you a communist."

"He just might. But this isn't material. It's a moral or spiritual value, or concept: the thing we used to have in the Talons about no killing."

Byron eyed him steadily but kept chewing.

"Yeah, no assaults at all. No injuries, at least to humans."

"I liked it, you know? The respect for another's existence. Sympathy for pain, distress. The idea was, if we killed or assaulted, we weren't any better than our adversaries."

"Uh-huh. But it seems that was unrealistic. We were using bombs, fire. It's like expecting an army to show surgical precision."

"I guess so. But we're moving along, now. The deaths or injuries won't be accidental. And they won't be animals, like last time."

"What are you saying? You think this project we're on might be wrong?"

Emmett inwardly drew back.

"No. I'm thinking killing is wrong, but it's justified here by the target's actions."

Byron nodded, and Emmett sensed a connection with him.

"Yeah," Byron said, "killing's justified a lot in society, even leaving out the wars. Self-defense, suicide, removing life supports, abortion maybe. Sometimes mercy killing."

"Then there's capital punishment."

"Right. That's what we're into *here*, isn't it?"

"Yes. Basically an execution, but more important for the message it sends. The target supports policies that cause widespread suffering, but his death can also stop others of like mind."

"Make an example of him."

"Right."

"I like it. Yeah, I think we've justified it."

* * *

Lying in bed later, waiting to sleep, Emmett thought of his wife Kirsten. She was at their home in Wisconsin, far from the present scene, so Emmett would have to handle this on his own. He'd think of Kirsten increasingly as he finished up with the Talons, picture her with their baby daughter in the small house outside Madison. They were as sheltered and secure as possible against a society stirred by hate and arrogance, religious and national fanaticism. It helped to have the buffer of the university community, though Emmett didn't consider himself a "liberal." He was simply committed to what made sense, what seemed necessary for his daughter as he watched her in her crib. He expressed this commitment in his work with the Talons. He knew he had a lot to lose, but he made this his reason to do things right.

4.

It was gray and misty when The Postman rapped on their door, advising them it was "go time." Emmett was at the wheel as they drove out of town and through a bucolic stretch to the point. They passed a country club, golf areas, and a state park, ending up on a blunt promontory fringed with a stony beach. Beyond lay the shrouded waters of Long Island Sound. The road ran parallel to the beach but Emmett stopped the van near the outmost growth of trees and bushes. Here, with the benefit of cover, they could strike at the helicopter flying from Wingham, up the coast, to the corporate studios in New York City. Dr. Lamont and The Postman, without the SAM today, proceeded into the cover while Byron acted as lookout. Emmett remained in the van, poised to drive off quickly. Though it was a mild day for winter, the dampness increased the chill that eddied along the coastline.

Sitting in the parked van, his window lowered for air, Emmett reflected on the moment. It had a spiritual quality, he and his comrades waiting in gray silence to view the evil they'd take down. It was a conflict of basic universal forces and he'd play a vital role, making his relationship to the others something more than political or fraternal. Somewhere in his mind, of course, was the little voice that continued to say, "But it's wrong to kill." What the little voice didn't know, however, or didn't care about, was that their target himself supported widespread killing and other evils. The Talons' act would therefore be a just execution, as well as something to protect humanity in the future.

The mechanical pulse of a helicopter rose from up the coast. Emmett tensed and peered out the open window, feeling somehow intimidated by the sound. It suddenly became much louder and its source could be seen, though blurred by fog, slicing toward New York City. It was a huge black insect, ugly but quickly gone.

Dr. Lamont and The Postman were walking briskly back to the van, talking earnestly. Byron followed from his vantage point, hands in pockets and looking cold. Emmett started the van and checked that the doors were unlocked. He delayed in using the headlights to avoid attracting notice.

"We'll return to the motel," said Lamont, "by a different route, more or less roundabout. We can just pass it today and go to breakfast, but tomorrow we go in and check out. In pairs again, with an interval in-between. Just a couple of business parties leaving."

"Any chance they might use a roadblock?" asked Byron.

"Not until well after we're gone. Anyway, the SAM components will be back at the point, in the bushes. We'll be clean as a church choir."

Emmett took the circuitous route prescribed by Lamont, who gave directions as he consulted a local map. Reaching the motel, they breezed on by and proceeded to a busy restaurant on the far side of town. After breakfast, Byron took the wheel and they visited a nature preserve, open year-round, where they could kill the rest of the morning.

"So," asked The Postman, "what're we supposed to be now? Bird-watchers?"

Dr. Lamont chuckled.

"Not a bad idea. But no, botanists is more believable. Just refer any questions to me."

They sauntered along the trail.

"You know," said The Postman, "this dude we're taking down, some parts of his show got nothing to do with corporate power. I mean, like celebrities on trial, or a husband killed his wife, a mom killed her kids. Stuff like that."

"Uh-huh," said Dr. Lamont, "and in doing that he reflects the treatment of news by his network. By giving endless attention to tabloid stories, he and the network divert attention from real issues. Ones that are 'inconvenient' to discuss. For the owners of the network, I mean, and other corporate types and their lackeys in government."

"The network," said Emmett, "would say they broadcast those stories because people *want* them, the celebrities and such."

"News as entertainment," Byron added.

"Sad but true," acknowledged Lamont. "But who was it that *conditioned* the viewing audience to that pablum? The usual suspects, right? Dishing out months of stories about one or two killings, or a celebrity rape, while ignoring the thousands being abused by our government."

"Conditioning, yeah," said The Postman. "They do that with 'American interests,' too. Like it's for *us* they bomb those weddings and hospitals in Iraq and Afghanistan. What garbage!"

"Misleading terminology, yes. The corporate media passes it right along. But we're supposed to be relaxing, gents. Seems our friends the trees aren't cutting it for us."

"I saw a pool hall when we were driving," Byron ventured.

"Great!" said Lamont. "We can spend the afternoon there, work the tree sap out of our lungs."

"Get the hell out of Walden Pond," smiled The Postman.

"Now, now. The place is serving its purpose: kill time without being conspicuous, get a little exercise. Somehow, I think Thoreau would've agreed with us."

They found their van and, buying sandwiches on the way, returned to their motel. After lunch, they rotated partners while playing two-on-two at the pool hall. Of the four of them, Dr. Lamont showed the most skill. Aggressive and precise, he with any partner would beat the opposing pair.

"Comes from being a chiropractor," he said. "All that time bending over the treatment table. I'm used to the position."

Though Emmett was sometimes bothered by Lamont's offhandedness, he admired the man's readiness for the next day's strike. Unlike himself, Lamont was apparently past the moral quandary on taking Hanlon's and the pilot's lives. He was free to enjoy playing pool as if they were, in fact, computer techies on an installation. Emmett wondered whether, in having his doubts, he was being a moral elitist. Perhaps what he saw as values were simply parts of a cherished self-concept that he was loath to give up. If so, it was mere selfishness that threatened to impede him. Emmett felt grateful to Dr. Lamont for helping him see this. Whatever their differences, he should be guided by the other's example on this project.

That evening, Emmett and Byron watched Dick Hanlon's show in their motel room. The news spinner was as arrogant as ever, oblivious to the fact that he was doing his last show. Emmett could have been amused by this, taking smug satisfaction, but instead he felt pity for the man. With a morning execution awaiting him, Hanlon persisted in his frenzied service to corrupt financial schemers. He railed against regulation, the United Nations, professors, and the non-religious. Byron got tired of it and went to take a shower, but Emmett stayed and heard a later segment concerning the Earth Freedom Force, from which two cells had split to join the Talons.

"Why *not* use the army against them?" insisted Hanlon. "Since local authorities can't do the job, or *won't*, give the scum a taste of *real* military force! And don't tell me about *Posse Comitatus*, Tenth Amendment, and the like. We're all Americans, aren't we? The EFF is our enemy, so send in the army!"

Emmett hit the mute button and watched Hanlon's mouth

working silently. He'd be talking against *habeas corpus*, calling for military tribunals, but Emmett was starting to feel the nausea that had driven Byron to the shower. Still, Emmett wanted to see the show to its end, to witness Hanlon's final performance in the series that merited his death. It was a necessary ritual, since any death was an issue for Emmett and had to be fully processed.

* * *

Waiting for sleep, Emmett was conscious of the divide between himself and Byron. The other knew his limitations, wouldn't stray out of his depth. He was content to remain an operative and was a good one. But Emmett saw things from another perspective. What about the human element here? Shouldn't they be concerned about the suffering the two deaths would cause others? He knew the answer the higher-ups would give, which Byron accepted without question: the real cause of the suffering was the evil the Talons were fighting–in which, actually, most of these others were participating. Emmett let it pass provisionally, since without the Talons he had no movement. But in his heart he would never accept killing, or reckless assault, as a means to an end. It would move him too close in spirit to the generals and politicians who worked for the corporate powers he despised.

* * *

The Postman brought coffee to their room next morning, Emmett letting him in while Byron was dressing.

"Twenty minutes," he said. "Everybody okay on this?"

"I'm fine," replied Emmett.

"No problem," Byron added.

The Postman nodded.

"We got good conditions. Everything's go. Me and Lamont'll be in the van. Time it to the minute."

"Right," said Emmett.

The mist was less dense than the day before, but the chill was somehow more penetrating. Maybe the caffeine, Emmett thought. He drove to the point by the same route, careful to observe all traffic laws. Nobody joked about his caution. They rode in near-silence, The Postman taking SAM components out of computer boxes. As Emmett heard the sounds, he gazed over the park and golf land that lined the road, imagined how the morning's peace would soon be shattered. Not our fault, he thought. It's a reaction to the shattered peace in other lands, and the shattering of lives here under arrogant policies. My daughter back home in her crib, her entire generation, depends on this action today to save our society. Some would say the *world* depends on it–the "global village"–all our destinies interconnected.

He parked the van and Byron got out to ascend his vantage point. He carried a walkie-talkie to warn of any problem. Once he was in place, Dr. Lamont and The Postman unloaded the missile round. They each gripped the leather shoulder strap, on opposite sides, and carried it low between them. The Postman cradled the gripstock in his free arm, while Dr. Lamont held the battery/cooling unit. Emmett watched as they disappeared into the furthest clump of substantial trees and bushes. From a distance, it would not have been clear what they were carrying. It could have been survey equipment or other tools. Yet, within minutes, The Postman would be poised to launch a stinger.

"It's not too late," said the little voice in Emmett's mind. "You can start the motor and drive quickly away, go all the way to Wisconsin. Or dump the van en route and take a plane or train. Forget you ever heard of the Talons or the Shortfall Club."

But Emmett answered that it couldn't happen. Besides the

repercussions of such an act, he was incapable of betraying his comrades at this point. Their escape and safety were in his hands, and they were risking their lives for a cause in which he passionately believed. The little voice was just a desperate prisoner in a defunct chamber of his brain. However evil this day might appear, what they were doing was necessary and good. Emmett could never live with himself if he failed to do his part.

In the distance, the thrumming of a helicopter began.

Emmett started the van's engine, searched the sky through its windows. The fog at first hid their quarry, but it soon emerged in dawn's refracted light. It was lacking the ugliness today, even taking on beauty for Emmett. His hand gripped the gearshift, his foot covering the brake.

The thrumming grew very loud, covering the sound of Emmett speeding away.

* * *

As the day passed, a park employee called the Newbridge P.D. to report finding the SAM among some bushes. A van was dispatched to the promontory on the Sound, where officers found the weapon ready for firing. It was dismantled and taken in for processing. The chief, who supplied the local newspaper with items for the "Police Blotter" feature, made a special call. The paper duly reported the find on its front page the following day, but the story was not picked up by major media. It apparently lacked significance in the eyes of those who decide such things.